THE GRANDPA STORIES

THE GRANDPA STORIES

TALES OF OTHERWORLDLY ADVENTURE

ROGER GRIMSON

authorHOUSE®

AuthorHouse™
1663 Liberty Drive
Bloomington, IN 47403
www.authorhouse.com
Phone: 1-800-839-8640

First published by AuthorHouse   12/28/2011

ISBN: 978-1-4678-7286-7 (sc)
ISBN: 978-1-4678-7287-4 (ebk)

Printed in the United States of America

This book is printed on acid-free paper.

This book is for my son, Randy; daughter, Julia; and two of my grandchildren, Alexi and Rachel.

I told bedtime stories to Randy and Julia many years ago, and they loved them and wanted to talk about them. That's when I learned that I have a yearning to make up fantasy fiction stories.

I also told bedtime stories to Alexi and Rachel, and when they were in their preteens and early teens, we had good times making up stories together. Alexi and Rachel are the models for Exi and Chel in these (no longer bedtime) stories.

CONTENTS

Foreword ix

Preface..xi

Acknowledgments xiii

Grandpa's Headaches 1

The Fishing Trip 18

Turning Visible 40

The Detectives...45

Molly 53

The Tenant 93

The Importance of Hitting the Target 100

Grandma's Dream: Orchids and Peacocks 119

Grandpa's Dream: The Curtain Rod 124

Bojangles 128

Mirror, Mirror on the Wall.. 143

The Secret about the Magic Shop 167

FOREWORD

The first time I met Roger Grimson was in an Olive Garden crowded with families, surrounded by friends of my uncle, who was up from Florida for a high school reunion. At the time, I was young and fairly shy, unwilling to jump into most of the conversations at the table. However, only six months earlier, I had been ecstatic to see the release of my first novel, *Light Years*, a self-published fantasy for teens; *that* was a subject I was eager to talk about with anyone who was interested. Roger was. He had an avid imagination, and his curiosity about my book—much of which was born from my own lifetime love for fantasy and magic—was flattering. Yet I didn't know then how much we truly had in common.

More than a year later, I received a phone call from Roger. To my surprise and delight, he informed me that he had written a book of his own, a collection of short stories that he wanted to self-publish, as I had. But most excitingly, he wanted *me* to edit it and provide feedback.

I agreed, and he sent me his manuscript shortly afterward. Before we began, however, Roger gave me one warning: the story lines he thought up were sometimes a bit bizarre. He himself admitted over the phone that he didn't know where he came up with many of his ideas. Though this warning certainly didn't turn me away from the project, it made me wary; once anything

I read begins to venture into the utterly eerie or goofy realms of fantasy's wide span, I have a tendency to put the work down.

Roger's stories, however, were nothing like that.

Remember when you were younger and believed that anything was possible? When adventures with fantastic treasures at the end waited behind every unknown door? When you still believed that there were fairies and unicorns hiding among the trees of the forest, but they were just too quick to catch? When magic tricks were still magical?

That age is the time *The Grandpa Stories* will transport you back to—a time when you still knew about the enchantments that existed out in the world, untouched by adult disbelief and just waiting to be discovered. Like most fantasy authors, Roger Grimson has not fully left that world behind. Unicorns, talking butterflies, invisibility potions, fantastic realms, and magical transformations run rampant through his stories, yet all are depicted through such clear and whimsical writing that they have the ability to reach through the pages and touch readers of all ages.

That land you once knew so well hasn't gone away. It's still out there, and it still hums with the beautiful magic of your childhood. And if you ever need reminding, pick up this book and slip down the rabbit hole for a little while; that charmed world will always be here waiting for you.

—Claudia Geib
Author, *Light Years* and *The Brushers*

PREFACE

I used to love telling nighttime fantasy stories to my children and grandchildren. But to my astonishment, some of the stories arose and loomed forward out of the cozy bedtime serenity, assumed a misty transparency, and floated throughout the room. Like clouds in the wind, they rolled and grew with complexity. They floated from the room and permeated the house—what a sight to witness! They shimmered though the rooms like veiled clues of "other worlds," dispersing hints of astounding adventures. Then they finally landed on these pages. The stories are for readers of all ages—except for tiny ones who want bedtime stories and may flinch at, say, the word "ghost" or the word "*boo!*"

Seemingly, we live in a world confined to the three spatial dimensions and one constant dimension of time. But certain episodes involving Grandpa, Grandma, and two of their grandchildren, Exi and Chel, curve deeply off these tracks and into other "worlds" not so confined—worlds with different kinds of time and space, and with connections with the world we know as Earth. They touch on the paranormal, the core of ultimate beauty, the way to paradise, goodness, evil, the unseen world within all mirrors, the voice of God, The Wonderful Place, and much more.

Grandpa is a magician. He makes a living performing magic and constructing products of magic in his shop for sell to the public. There is a vast difference, however, between such magic and the profound paranormal events that have absolutely nothing to do with sleight of hand, which you are to witness in these stories. Curiously, in a few cases, human magic and the paranormal do interact—with explosive results!

ACKNOWLEDGMENTS

I wish to thank Claudia Geib (see the foreword) for reading the manuscript and making many helpful suggestions and editorial recommendations, and for the many hours of conversation we had about the book and related matters.

Also, I wish to show my appreciation to Melissa Eatman Grimson and Brittany Farrell for reading the draft and making several useful suggestions.

GRANDPA'S HEADACHES

"The procedure is simple," the surgeon said. "We'll drill a small hole in the top of your skull and insert a needle-thin tube down into the center of your brain. Through the tube, we'll insert a microscope that's so small that you can't see it with the naked eye. Then, with the aid of digital enhancement equipment, we'll look through the tube and scan all components in the core of your brain to see if we can find any anomaly that's causing your headaches. You won't feel a thing. Do you have any questions?"

"No, no. Thanks, Doc. Okay. See ya tomorrow." Grandpa was overwhelmed as he stood up to leave Dr. Clark's office.

The next morning, Grandma was in the waiting room, praying for a successful surgery and a treatment for Grandpa's headaches. The headaches were predictable. They would start with a bang and last for maybe an hour. He had them on a regular basis, twice a day, once in the morning and once in the afternoon.

Chel and Exi returned to the waiting room after visiting the hospital's gift shop. "Look, Grandma. We got Grandpa a surprise for when he wakes up."

Grandma looked inattentively toward the girls, not really thinking about anything except Grandpa, when in a flash she seemed to awake with a smile. "Oh! Grandpa will love it!"

The girls held up a small clear glass unicorn with her head held high to the sky, with three legs evenly secured to the ground and her right front leg pulled up to her chest with the hoof pointed downward. Her tail was beautifully outstretched, enhancing the stature of the figurine. But there was an unusual feature that distinguished the figurine from most others: embedded inside her glass head was a colorful globe of the world.

"The lady in the gift shop said that if you look through the unicorn's glass head at the globe using a magnifying glass, you can see that the details of the world are exact," Chel said.

The girls carefully rewrapped it in its tissue, placed it back in the box, slid the ribbon around it, and combined their heads to write a note to Grandpa.

◊

Using the latest neurological equipment, Dr. Clark had been scoping Grandpa's brain for several minutes. He peered up at the assisting surgeon and handed her the viewing apparatus of the brain scope. "Joan, I want you to take a look at this."

Dr. Joan Meson guided the scope throughout the region that Dr. Clark had been viewing.

"Do you see what I see?" Dr. Clark asked.

"I think so, but what is it? It looks like some kinda . . . wonderland . . . from a storybook or something."

Dr. Clark beckoned to the technician in charge of recordkeeping for future research. "Please record the following. At location coordinate .00520334, .00418497, .00230115, near the absolute center of the patient's brain, we see extraordinarily unusual activity at the most powerful microscopic level. We see what looks like another world. There are beautiful trees that bear varieties of fruits and what looks like colorful candies. We see yellow and silver structures that mushroom up from the ground, but unlike mountains, they do not stop rising. They seem to blend with a gorgeous silver sky, laced with swirls of yellows, pinks, and other colors. Unicorns float through the air. Higher in the sky, we see kangaroos moving as if paddling on air in slow motion. Huge colorful butterflies dominate the landscape. Beautiful lakes and rolling orchards are spread throughout this place. Sounds bizarre but we're just trying to accurately record what we see. Enough for now."

Grandma and the girls were sitting silently when Dr. Clark entered the waiting room to give them the post-surgery update. "Roger is resting and doing fine. The surgery went well. There were no complications. However, unfortunately, we could find no anomaly usually associated with headaches."

"Is there no way to stop the headaches?" Grandma pleaded.

"I don't know. Usually we can identify the source and correct it. This case is puzzling. However, I have to tell you that we did find something extraordinary. We tried to film it for the formal record, but evidently, only the human eye is able to process what we saw in Grandpa's brain."

As Dr. Clark began to describe what he and Dr. Meson saw in Grandpa's brain, Exi immediately recognized the description. "That's The Wonderful Place!" she cried aloud.

Instinctively, her hands covered her mouth. No one on Earth except her sister and grandparents knew about The Wonderful Place. The secrecy was for its protection. Revealing the existence of this supreme place of beauty and wonder could result in harm to it.

In that split second, Exi pictured her last visit there. Exi and Chel were sitting comfortably on the back of an extraordinary and friendly life-form, flying, swerving in easy arcs, and rising and diving calmly. They were viewing the remarkable beauty of their recently discovered new world.

"The verticals!" Exi exclaimed, looking deep into the distance. "Let's see if she'll fly us to a vertical. We've never seen one up close."

Verticals comprised a source of beauty and awe for the Wonderlites, the inhabitants of that amazing place. Some were yellow in color, and the others were silver. They were larger around than giant redwood trees; some were larger around than an enormous building.

Verticals came up from the ground as trees do, and near the ground, they had what resembled roots. These were ground flares. For the larger verticals, the ground flares began to branch off from the vertical about fifteen feet above ground level and spread out as they descended, until they sank into the ground thirty feet away. Other than these similarities, they were far different from trees.

The massive structures seemingly never stopped rising from their foundations. Hundreds of miles into the sky, they burst into rainbows of spectacular colors, softly floating and reaching across the sky like giant streamers. Some streamers sparkled, and once in a special while, a tiny dazzling speck would part from its sparkle and curve down to give you a gentle kiss on the cheek. Then it would soar back up to its orbit, all within a few seconds. Such an occurrence would become a rare and treasured memory. The Wonderful Place was alive and loved its inhabitants.

Exi and Chel had discovered The Wonderful Place two years ago. They had been playing by the giant oak in back of the parking lot, behind Grandpa's magic shop. The tree had quite a history. No one knew its age. It had a girth larger than any oak in the state, according to an old report published in a nature magazine. It was also the tallest tree in the state. For a short while after the report appeared, a few curious people drove by for a look. A botanist once spent half a day studying the tree and taking various bark and interior samples for a research project. He could not get all the way to the core because the tree was too massive. He finally concluded that there was nothing special about the tree except the obvious: it was enormous.

Grandpa didn't mind this activity while it lasted, because some of the curious viewers also noticed Grandpa's magic shop and went in for a visit. People still occasionally commented on the size of the tree.

But Exi, Chel, Grandma, and Grandpa knew something about the tree that no one else in the world would ever even dream of. This secret rested in the tree's center. The tree, starting just above the roots, had a twenty-foot diameter. Although the tree narrowed as it progressed skyward, its center was a passageway with a narrow stairway spiraling up the circular walls. The stairwell was about six feet in diameter and never narrowed, even after exceeding the height of the tree; from inside the tree the stairwell continued upward for several tree lengths, but from outside the tree the stairwell does not exist.

In a flash, she recalled a conversation she'd recently had with Grandpa at the magic shop about how she and Chel discovered the secret of the giant oak—and ultimately, The Wonderful Place. "Yeah, Grandpa, the big roots came out like arms of a giant starfish. Chel and I would go there and dig between the roots for earthworms for Grandma for her fishing trips to the lake. The worms were big there. We found out about them when the spaniel next door would dig 'em up. We were next to the part of the trunk that was facing the back of your shop when we heard thumping sounds. Between two roots, there was a cavern about six feet long into the tree, large enough for a person to squeeze into. The sounds came from there. We'd just started to go closer when, from the back of the cavern, a door squeaked open. The door was deep enough into the cavern and blended in so well with the tree that we never even knew it was there—for all these years!"

Exi paused in the conversation with Grandpa, glanced through the back window at the tree, and then looked back to Grandpa again. "Chel and I were scared. We just froze. We couldn't see how that could be."

"But it was. Exi, there are many strange and mysterious things in our world, many yet to be discovered," Grandpa said in his philosophical manner.

Exi continued. "We heard something crawling toward us through the cavern. As we backed away a head appeared. It looked like a horse's head at first, but it had a long horn. I remember how frightened we were. And she was startled when she saw us. She lifted her head and turned it slightly so we could see only one huge round red eye looking at us, sizing us up. For a moment, the three of us were frozen in space. Finally, she moved. She smiled and wiggled herself out of the cavern of the tree. We saw her wings. She was beautiful."

Thus, for the first time ever, intelligent beings from two different worlds met. This encounter initiated a long and close friendship between four Earth people—Exi, Chel, and their grandparents—and the inhabitants of The Wonderful Place.

"Hi," the flying unicorn said. "My name is Uni."

"Hi, I'm Exi."

"And I'm Chel."

Uni related the events that led to her appearance on Earth. The existence of the trapdoor at the roots of a sweet tree growing in The Wonderful Place was not known until she found it and opened it a few minutes earlier. It rested slightly below ground level of The Wonderful Place and was partially obscured by the labyrinth of roots of the sweet tree. The sweet tree was much smaller than the giant oak on Earth. It appeared that the giant oak (only from the stairwell inside) grew right up to the trapdoor at the base of the sweet tree.

The fruits of the sweet tree were delicious and the flavors varied; they were better than any candy the girls ever tasted on Earth, yet they were nutritious. Later, when the girls visited The Wonderful Place, each would pick up a fallen fruit and devour it. The girls called it a lollipop tree. The trunk and branches were purple, and the hanging leaves glowed with every color imaginable.

That's where Exi and Chel would meet Uni, climb onto her back, and soar off on one of their adventures in The Wonderful Place.

◊

Back in the hospital, Exi's exclamation left Dr. Clark puzzled.

"What?" the doctor asked, turning toward Exi.

"Oh, it sounds like a wonderful place," Exi said, correcting herself instantly.

"Well, we don't know what it is but we plan to do some research to find out more about this phenomenon, with Grandpa's permission. Tentatively, we are speculating that this is related to the imagination, or dream center, of the brain."

Grandma inquired. "You mean, maybe Grandpa was imagining or dreaming about all this while you were exploring his brain? And you could see it? You discovered how to see someone else's imaginations or dreams?"

"Possibly," Dr. Clark replied reservedly. "However, if we go by what we see, then Grandpa has another real, three-dimensional world existing deep in his brain. Four dimensions counting time, because living things are moving around, and that requires time. That's the observation. We can only speculate that we were seeing what was being imagined or dreamed. Otherwise, he would have some kind of unusual world in his brain."

"Does Grandpa know?" Grandma asked.

"Not yet. I will tell him after he has rested. You all have a nice day."

On their way home, Grandma and the girls talked about Grandpa's unusual situation. At one point, Grandma heard the sudden giggle-talk from the girls, recognizing the coincidental similarity between what was in Grandpa's brain and the glass unicorn with the globe of the world in her head.

◊

The next day, the afternoon was sunny and warm. Grandpa was recuperating on his recliner in the fresh outdoor air of the screened garden porch they'd named the "Rainbow Room". When Exi and Chel came over with a glass of iced tea for Grandpa, he was smiling.

Grandpa was thinking that if The Wonderful Place was really inside his head, then something going on there might be related to his headaches. He was reflecting on some strange activity he thought he saw from a distance the last time he was there—and simultaneously experienced a headache.

"I think I've figured out what's causing my headaches."

"What?" the girls asked in unison.

"We'll find out together in a few days when I'm feeling stronger. We'll go to The Wonderful Place. I have a mission, and I want you girls to come with me and meet Uni there in case I need help—and to witness whatever happens. In the meantime, I'm not speculating any further. I want to think this through more thoroughly."

Grandpa's expression deepened. "Exi, tomorrow I want you to go to the tree and leave this message for

Uni at the cubby hole at the top of the stairs. You know where it is."

"Sure, Grandpa. No problem."

That Saturday, Grandpa and the girls were ready. Not much preparation was required for visiting The Wonderful Place. It was not necessary to bring drinking water, because the bountiful springs offered the purest, coolest water possible. And one could spend days picking and eating healthy foods and desserts that nature provided everywhere. Comfortable clothes and shoes were all that were required, usually. This time, Grandpa did have one extra requirement.

"Exi, go to the shed and bring me the ax please —*carefully*."

The three explorers climbed with the ax up the spiral stairway inside the huge oak. At the top, they opened the door at the base of the giant lollipop tree. They crawled out once again into the gorgeous land of tranquility, carefully stepping over a small patch of gumdrop mushrooms reaching up toward them from the tree's fruity roots. The visitors were blown a welcoming kiss by a pink-and-yellow kangaroo gliding nearby.

These kangaroos were spectacular creatures when seen up close as well as when seen dotting the far sky. They were multicolored, often blending with the colorful sky, their coats exhibiting pleasing geometric or strikingly irregular patterns. Some sported colorful wavering bands separating otherwise bright white coats. Others were speckled—like moons and suns against a light purple night sky.

Reflecting on the seemingly unusual activity he'd witnessed at a distance during his last visit, coinciding with the onset of a headache, Grandpa thought, *These beautiful and kind kangaroos . . . Could they innocently be causing my headaches?*

Uni had received Grandpa's message and arrived as requested. "I have the information you asked for, Roger," Uni said.

"Thank you, Uni. We'll talk about that in a little while."

Meanwhile, the suspense was growing for the girls.

Grandpa abruptly reminded himself of the mission. "Girls, Uni, point to the nearest vertical."

Since Exi and Chel had discovered The Wonderful Place, they, Grandma, and Grandpa had had wondrous adventures there, becoming acquainted with the Wonderlites, understanding their ways of life and their driven questions, such as the questions about the verticals, for example. The sky seemed indistinguishable from the distant parts of the verticals. This was the basis of one of the most profound scientific and philosophical mysteries concerning the Wonderlites. It was in their nature to understand their greater environment. Did the upper reaches of the verticals actually fan out and comprise the sky? Or was the sky separate from the verticals and much higher? This was an important question. Some Wonderlites believed that the verticals eventually became the sky and thus comprised one magnificent canopy of beauty. Others believed that the verticals visually blended in with the sky and contributed to its beauty, but that the sky was separate from, and much higher than, the reaches of the verticals.

"That one over there," Chel said, pointing to a vertical about half a mile away.

"Okay, we're off," Grandpa said, resting his ax on his shoulder and taking his first dedicated step.

The vertical had little ground flare; it extended outward twenty feet, which was on the short side.

When the four reached the vertical, Exi placed her hand on it. "It's so smooth and slightly soft."

"I'm glad it's soft," Grandpa said. "I'm going to whack it with the ax. This is my opportunity to test my theory."

Grandpa explained to the girls and Uni that they should stand back and pay attention, remembering everything that happened.

With one swift swing, he sank the ax head deep into the vertical.

Instantly, he writhed in pain and held his head. After a few seconds, the pain abated somewhat, leaving him with a mild headache. A small amount of red liquid oozed out of the spot where the ax met the ground flare of the vertical.

"I proved my theory!" Grandpa announced with great satisfaction.

"Okay, *now* will you explain to us what's going on?" Chel demanded.

"I have just axed the interior of my brain. The Wonderful Place is inside my brain. Two surgeons are witnesses."

"Grandpa!" Chel interjected. "That makes no sense. You are *in* The Wonderful Place. Not the other way around."

Exi agreed. "Yeah, that would mean that all of us standing here are also standing in the middle of your brain."

"You got it!" Changing focus, Grandpa asked, "Uni, what did you find out?"

Uni related to Grandpa the results of her research. "Your theory is correct, Grandpa. The kangaroos indeed were planning to find out more about the verticals; they wanted a better understanding of our world. In fact, a few weeks ago, they began to make a tunnel into the center of one to see what's there. But it proved to be slow going. They could only work for an hour at a time because after an hour, so much red stuff would spill out that they would have to quit until everything dried up. So they worked for an hour in the morning and an hour in the afternoon. Two hours a day."

"Those times correspond to the times of my headaches," Grandpa said. "Are you girls beginning to see?"

Exi related another conflict. "The Wonderful Place has been around forever, way before you were born. It should last after you die. None of this makes sense, Grandpa. Before you were conceived, you had no brain, so The Wonderful Place couldn't have been there."

Grandpa finally had to say something on the subject, although he was no expert. "Have you ever heard of dual existences or parallel universes? Everything we know is made of matter. Some scientists say that there has to be a balance in the universe: antimatter. For every existence, there is a duplicate antimatter existence. I don't understand the details but . . ."

The girls didn't buy it. "That's too simplistic for this situation, Grandpa."

Grandpa turned to Uni. "My headaches will stop when the kangaroos stop excavating the vertical."

"I've already spoken with them about your theory," Uni said. "In fact, they did not think it was farfetched, you may be interested to know. Kangaroos have keen intuitions about things, and they are curious philosophers. They said that they would stop the exploration if that's what's causing your headaches. They told me that if that's the case, they might not need to carry on the excavations because probably all they would need is a description from your surgeons as to what they saw at the upper end of the verticals. Even if the surgeons can't see where the verticals go, they'll still stop this excavation and try to find some other way to solve the mystery."

Grandpa responded, "They'll have a written explanation within the week. I'll be here to give it to them. Please thank them for me." Before he turned to go, he added, "Great work, Uni. Really great work. Thank you."

Then he gestured to his granddaughters. "Girls, thank you. I love you. It's time to go home."

◊

Grandpa felt relaxed. It had been a productive day. For the first time in days, he felt freely speculative. "Isn't it great that solutions can be found for problems even when no one has a *full* understanding of fundamental underlying details?"

"If that weren't the case, Grandpa, then nothing would ever get accomplished. The telephone is just one of a billion examples," Exi said, displaying tremendous insight.

But Grandpa had a craving for an understanding of the day's events. *How on earth can The Wonderful Place be inside me, and I be standing in The Wonderful Place at the same time?* he wondered.

That night when Grandpa went to bed, he could not sleep, although the night was silent. "Thank you, kangaroos," he said softly to himself as he kept mulling over the day's events. Grandpa had always been a man of great curiosity; he felt blessed with that. But being blessed hard enough with something can be akin to being cursed by it. He knew he was able to solve his headache problem whereas the surgeons could not, although, indirectly, they contributed. But he felt limited in understanding the how and why of things.

He whispered his lonely defeat: "I just can't grasp how I can be in a place and have that place inside me at the exact same time."

A voice emerged from the shadows. "I can."

Grandpa's first thought was that it was Grandma, but it wasn't her voice. She was sound asleep.

Moonlight barely lit the room. Grandpa turned away from Grandma and looked in the direction he thought the voice came from. No one was there. He was looking too high, toward the door. A glitter of light lowered his line of sight toward the nightstand. Facing him a few inches away, eye-to-eye, was the little glass unicorn with the whole wide world in her head.

The Fishing Trip

T HE SEA WAS CALM, and a cloudless blue sky surrounded the midday sun. Grandpa and his two granddaughters were deep-sea fishing on *The Vault's Keeper*, Grandpa's proud old fishing boat. They had been fishing for more than two hours with no luck, but their luck was about to change, in a most peculiar way.

"Maybe we should break for lunch," Grandpa moaned, facing the sun.

"What does *The Vault's Keeper* mean, Grandpa?" Exi asked.

"Oh!" Grandpa perked up. "Do you know what a vault is?"

"Yes."

"It's like a safe," Grandpa continued, beginning to reel in his fishing line. "A private protective box for valuable treasures or secret stuff. A vault's keeper, therefore, is one who is responsible for the security and maintenance of the vault."

"I guess what I meant, Grandpa, is why is the boat named *The Vault's Keeper*?"

"Well, because this boat contains a large hidden vault that may contain profound secrets and treasures," Grandpa explained.

"So?" queried Chel.

"Can you keep a secret?" The girls nodded silently, and Grandpa began to explain. "The vault is buried deep in the lowest place in the hull of the boat. And frankly, I don't even know what's in it. I've been trying to find a way to open it. The vault is ironclad and very old. Older than the boat. I think the boat was built around the vault. Actually, I am the vault's keeper because I own the boat, but I know nothing of the vault's secrets. As a professional magician, I should be able to find out how to open it. I've been working on it."

Grandpa straightened to rise out of the chair and repeated, "Let's break for lunch."

Then he paused and folded back into the chair, recalling the interesting history of the boat—as far as he knew it. "Grandma's father, your great-grandfather, Gudmunder the Viking, as they called him, was the second owner of *The Vault's Keeper*. He was a true boatman. Knowledge of the first owner is lost in time. The only possible clue of any previous owner is an inscription carved in the wall of the narrow stairwell that leads below the deck to the vault: 'The Great Serge.' An old tale had it that the boat simply appeared, empty, on a calm, clear sea one day several decades back. Gudmunder soon thereafter bought it at an auction."

Grandpa looked at Exi and Chel, taking note of their quiet attention. "Girls, a remarkable tragedy happened on this boat. One day in nineteen fifty, Gudmunder sailed out into the ocean and disappeared forever. A few days later, the boat was found adrift, again, with no signs of life on it. Those were tough times for the family. Grandma eventually inherited *The Vault's Keeper*. We modernized it and had a small motor put in it so as not to rely only on the sails. Grandma gave the boat to me, and now I use it for fishing. The two of us used to take the boat out and fish together, but now she doesn't even want to come near the boat. She says she knows much more about the boat's secrets, but not enough . . . Whatever that means. I believe her, but it's her secret."

Grandpa always felt that Grandma possessed some paranormal abilities to which she would never admit. Grandpa had none, but he knew magic. However, even his magical prowess, which he sometimes used to solve mysteries, had not yet succeeded in affording him the discovery of the boat's secrets.

Exi and Chel were left with an earful to ponder as Grandpa went to the cooler to prepare lunch. They opened the door leading to stairs that descended into the hull, only to see darkness. They found a light switch and flicked it. The two then ambled down into the bowels of the boat to examine the vault. The vault was about six feet long and four feet wide and situated in the center of the floor. It resembled the top of a large treasure chest coming up through the bottom of the boat, leaving the chamber of the chest hanging downward into the ocean.

Exi and Chel knelt beside the chest, examining it, feeling it with their hands and fingers. "Look, here are some hinges on one side," Exi said. "But there's no latch or anything on the other side, like on most chests. No keyhole, no nothing."

Chel stood up and took a step back. "There has to be a way to open it. It doesn't make sense to have hinges and not be able to open it."

The two devised a meticulous plan to search the interior of the hull for any clue leading to a way of opening the vault. They would begin at the vault and work away from it, searching every square foot of space on the floor and walls.

During lunch, they explained their plan to Grandpa and asked him if he knew of something that they could draw with. "We want to be exact and not miss a thing that could lead to a way of opening the vault. There's got to be a way. So for each square foot of floor we explore, we'll draw a box around it to signal that we have already searched that area. We won't give up until each square foot area of the hull is boxed. The floor, the walls . . ."

"Great plan." Grandpa was nicely surprised by the intricate idea. "I think there's some thick carpenters chalk in a tool bin below—in the rear of the hull." He reached for his fishing gear. "You two work on that. I'll be fishing."

The tool bin was built into the boat. The girls flung open the lid and began rummaging around for the chalk. They removed a hammer, an adjustable wrench, and several other larger tools in their search. Stirring around the various other objects in the bin, they did not see the chalk, so they simply removed everything from the bin. Reaching half an arm's length in to feel the bottom, Exi asked Chel to hand her the flashlight. She wiped the grimy floor of the tool bin with a rag and discovered that the floor of the bin contained a tiny hole off to one side.

Exi immediately exclaimed, "The floor of the tool bin is actually a lid covering an even lower hidden compartment!"

Exi asked Chel for the thin awl that they had removed from the bin. Inserting it through the hole and twisting it, she lifted the floor of the bin up and away. She gasped and then cried out, "We found it!"

The girls discovered an old iron latch protruding toward them from the lower compartment. It was a thin bar about six inches long and curled on the near end for a finger hold, begging to be pulled.

Continuing to explore the newly discovered mysterious compartment under the tool bin with the flashlight, something else caught their eyes. The back side of the floor of the bin did not quite reach the back wall of it, leaving a gap about one inch wide running along the back. Shoved tightly in this space, they saw what appeared to be some crumpled parchment—a pouch, perhaps. But their struggles to free it were to no avail.

"*Grandpa, Grandpa!*" the two girls screamed, scrambling up the stairs in long strides. "We found it! We found it!"

"What's that?" Grandpa asked, watching his float. Grandpa, unlike most deep-sea fishermen, used a large float to hold the line and hook under the water, as often used in lake fishing to place the hook at desired levels below the surface. He liked to see and feel the softball-sized float bob and disappear beneath the surface. He yearned for the catch.

"The way to get into the vault!" the girls screamed in unison. They scrambled toward Grandpa, telling him how they had found a latch, and that there was something else important there, referring to what they assumed was a pouch.

Grandpa reeled in his line, put his rod down, and faced the girls. "Great job, girls! Show me."

Once within the hull, Grandpa glowed at the impressive sight. "This latch must be the way; it must be rigged up to the vault by some mechanism under the floor."

Using a pair of pliers and a screwdriver, he carefully worked the mysterious pouch out. It appeared to contain some loose heavy objects.

"Girls, let's go back on deck, where there's better light, and see what we have here. Let's go think this through," Grandpa suggested.

Sitting at the small circular lunch table on deck, Grandpa slid the contents out of what was indeed a pouch. The pouch was made from an old piece of parchment with some writing on it, but the contents were what especially caught their attention: two larger than average keys. The keys appeared to be ancient and were lavishly scrolled with unusual symbols. "Wow!" Grandpa exclaimed. "I have never seen such unusual, intricate, and ornate symbols."

Oh, look here," Exi interrupted. "Among all these symbols, a large circle is engraved on the handle of this key, and two large circles are engraved on the handle of the other."

The three then directed their attention to the writing, which was addressed "To the owner of *The Vault's Keeper.*" Grandpa cleared his throat and read aloud.

"Once you open the vault, you will see a vast space, larger than the boat itself. Although this seems impossible, it is real. You are about to enter a strange yet wonderful dimension of the universe. Once inside the vault, the lid will close and you will be sealed inside. There is only one way out of the vault. You will need to open two doors. The key with the single circle will get you through the first door, out of the vault and into a long corridor. Walking through the corridor, you will eventually come to another door. Use the key engraved with two circles to open this door. There you will receive the most precious treasure of your life, and you will be free. But be warned: the pair of keys is the only way out.

Without the keys, you and even your soul are doomed to remain inside the vault forever.

"A great treasure for *me*?" Grandpa softly pondered. "I'll share it with you two."

"Let's go," the girls said in unison.

"Let's go," Grandpa said.

They grabbed a hammer, a sharp chisel, a hand drill and bits, and other tools that they figured they would need in case they had to break out through the vault's lid once it closed behind them—if indeed they could. They also carried a flashlight and some water.

The lid sprang open when Grandpa pulled the latch. "Spring-loaded. I thought so." Grandpa was the first to climb down a short ladder to the base of the vault, and true to the written word, the lid slammed shut.

"Oh my God!" cried Exi. "Grandpa's down there alone."

The girls ran back to the latch and yanked the lid open again.

"What a start. You two climb down together." Grandpa always responded to a crisis with a plan.

The girls entered, and the lid closed behind them. The closed, locked room was dark and unwelcoming. The flashlight showed debris littering the floor; on one side of the vault's interior, the rubbish was piled particularly high. The flashlight beamed upon a human skull leaning up against the wall, and then it showed the rest of the skeleton unfolded outward toward them.

All three jumped back in shock at the foreboding sight. They scrambled up the ladder and found that the vault's lid remained tightly closed. *What have we gotten ourselves into?* Grandpa thought as the girls quivered.

"Look, it's not alive," Grandpa finally said. "So what's to fear? Hey, don't forget we have a plan." He turned to face the first door. "The passageway. And let's leave the heavy tools here, but we'll bring the flashlight just in case. Who has the keys?"

"You do, don't you, Grandpa?"

"Oh no! Oh," Grandpa said, patting down his pockets. "Okay, here they are." He dragged them out. The key inscribed with the single circle worked; Grandpa unlocked the door.

"We shouldn't change anything. We shouldn't leave this first door open." Grandpa carefully checked to see that the other side of the door had a keyhole, and that the key could turn the lock on that side too. They then closed the door behind them and locked it, beginning their journey.

◊

The corridor was well lit, though no lighting source was visible. It had no end in sight. The air was fresh and cool. The floor seemed to be paved in gold, and the walls and ceiling were a soft yellow color of some unknown material. But the completely captivating part of the corridor was that the walls and ceiling were majestically mounted with keys. Thousands of magnificent keys of all sizes and shapes covered the walls and ceiling, extending as far down the corridor as they could see.

Most of the keys were the same general shape as a classic skeleton key, and they were old and large—some over a foot long. Some pointed forward, some backward. Some pointed up, some down, and others were oriented at other angles. Their placements on the walls and ceiling comprised interesting, sometimes intricate, geometric configurations. The keys were a metallic hue. Some were silver, and others ranged from light gray to black. Many were inlaid with gold. The keys were somehow compelling, as if offered to the three travelers by the hands of one from another world—a world of untold mystery and, inexplicably, a world hinting of a degree of beauty not experienced on Earth.

Grandpa tried to photograph the sight using his cell phone, but the image was blank, as it was when Exi and Chel tried.

The three began strolling down the corridor, carefully studying their surroundings. They walked in silence for many minutes. Chel was the first to speak.

"What does all this mean?"

Grandpa responded, "I don't know, but so far, between the filthy vault and this remarkable corridor, this has been an amazing experience. I can't imagine what might be behind the next door."

"I'll bet that the skeleton was Gudmunder's," Chel remarked.

"Who knows," Exi said. "There was the other guy too, *Serge*."

Grandpa was quick to remind them that "Serge" was only a name carved into a wooden wall of the boat. "We may have solved an important mystery, if nothing else. Gudmunder's disappearance and the boat being found adrift is consistent with the notion that he found the latch and climbed into the chamber, but that he overlooked the pouch containing the keys and the message. The lid closed on him, and there he stayed for all these years."

Eventually, they arrived at a place in the corridor where ten especially long, sturdy keys protruded straight out from the right side of the wall, forming an enticing staircase leading upward. Smaller keys were interlaced to form an elaborate yet sturdy handrail. This led up to another complex of keys embedded in the ceiling. Here they witnessed a spectacle—hundreds of keys were set in a realistic-appearing formation of a golden trap door, complete with hinges, a latch, and a keyhole.

The three studied the wonderful and intricate pattern of keys for a minute. Then they continued their journey as planned, viewing other spectacular arrangements.

In due course, they paused to drink some water and to turn around to face the direction they had come from, just to see what it looked like. It looked just like the way they were going.

"Careful. Let's not get turned around. We have no compass." Grandpa wasn't joking. Then he wondered aloud, "Would one even work here at all?"

Eventually, they arrived at the final door. Grandpa examined the key with two circles. He then raised it above his face as if making an offering. The girls watched with their faces similarly lifted. In one swift motion, he lowered the key and unlocked the door. Leaning forward, Grandpa again checked to see if the key opened this door too from the other side, in case they found that they needed to return. Then he turned and faced ahead.

"Beautiful!" Chel whispered, peering from around Grandpa's back.

The three immediately found themselves softly floating through vast space, yet this sudden change from their standing at the door did not leave them in shock; they felt comfortable. After some reflection, they sensed that unknown powers were gently lifting and cradling them. They were enjoying this experience. Little light existed; it was not completely dark, but they did not see a moon or stars, as would be seen from Earth at nightfall. Bright yellow, red, and orange globes of varying sizes and shades fashioned the discernible distances, forming a heavenly panorama. Some globes brightened and dimmed. Twice, while they were experiencing travel in this phenomenally unusual space, they witnessed a multicolored arc of brilliant colors—colors of the rainbow. These curves of color slowly faded in, curved halfway around them, and pleasantly brightened before fading out. But there was no planet nor sun nor rain nearby, which are required for ordinary rainbows to exist. They knew that they were not just floating in the universe as we know it; they knew they were in some other mysterious celestial realm. Soon they felt comfortably aware (though they did not know why) that their treasure was seconds away.

◊

Grandma was sitting among the colorful floral arrangements in a corner of the Rainbow Room. She was crocheting a blanket when the three travelers tumbled out of the adjacent corner flowerpot cabinet and spilled flat out onto the tiled Rainbow Room floor.

"How goes the fishing?" Grandma smiled as she kneeled and embraced her family. Exi and Chel recognized Grandpa's treasure: Grandma.

Grandpa's blinking eyes dashed alternately from Grandma's smile to random points in the Rainbow Room, and when his bewilderment began to recede, he marveled at the thought that the three of them had traveled through a rainbow and had just reached its end.

Exi and Chel hugged Grandma. "You are our treasure too," Exi said.

Chel agreed and hugged her again.

Grandpa sat up and faced Grandma, realizing that the awkward emergence onto the Rainbow Room floor was of no surprise to her. The brief thought that she possessed some paranormal abilities that even he did not have gave him a moment's unease. Then he rested in the comfort of knowing that while she possessed certain limited psychic abilities to see and know things beyond the veil, she could not actually conduct magic, which was his province.

He smiled at her and confessed, "I'm glad it's over, and I'm glad it's *you*." Grandpa recognized this as a defining moment in his life. The exciting but admittedly traumatizing adventure was over. "Thank you, Lord!"

"It's not over," Grandma said, looking up and facing the opposite end of the Rainbow Room. "We have a visitor. My father! He traveled here much faster than you three humans, after you opened the doors for him." Grandma smiled and made the introduction with an opening motion of her arm.

"Thank you for opening the doors of a spirit's trap." Gudmunder's faint voice came from the direction of the swinging chair, moaning on its hinges, at the other end of the Rainbow Room. Grandpa and the girls gaped in that direction in sheer disbelief.

They saw that the chair held a wavering transparent human-like form . . . a ghost!

"Thank you for setting me free." Gudmunder's voice was hollowed and sweet, as though it floated from afar on the notes of a well-honed wooden flute. To each of his four viewers, his image was captivating; it was like peering into peaceful waves of reflecting water—with a human shape. Otherwise, it did not move, other than the slight motion from the breeze-blown chair. "I won't be here long. But you should know what happened."

Gudmunder related a most unusual and tragic experience. One time many years ago, he sailed his boat far out on the ocean. Adventure was what he sailed for. The weather was accommodating, and the boat happily responded to the sea and breeze like no other boat he had ever sailed. After a while, he loosened the ropes, furled the sails, and broke for a restful float, away from it all, on the high sea. After some peaceful rest on deck, he thought about the mystery of the vault buried in the hull.

Down below, pondering the vault and exploring the hull, he found the latch and pulled it, but he never saw the hidden pouch that contained the keys. He witnessed the lid separate from the top of the vault, and then, using his lantern, he peered down into its dark crevasse. His eyes adjusted to the darkness, and he crawled in. The lid closed. His physical body died, but his spirit lived immortally there for well over half a century.

"The vault is the embodiment of pure evil. Without the keys, even the soul is doomed," Gudmunder explained. "But I'm not the only one," Gudmunder added. "You also freed Serge, who will introduce himself shortly. The skeleton you saw was mine. His was older and better concealed. And the three of you rushed right out after seeing mine."

Surveying the eyes of his daughter and great-grandchildren Gudmunder said, "It's wonderful seeing you. I love you. Good-bye." And he disappeared.

The breeze intensified; branches shifting against the late afternoon sun created dancing shadows in the Rainbow Room. Chel had to squint for a second look; she peered through the open door leading into the house and discovered, occupying the space within the frame and slightly wavering, a vague humanlike form.

"I have one thing I must reveal, and I too must be brief," Serge faintly said. "I also missed the pouch. How lucky the three of you were. I discovered the boat, and I was its first known owner. I was fishing off the beach at daybreak one morning when the boat simply appeared a few hundred yards in front of me. It emerged, like a sailfish, bow first, up out of the water, and then flattened out on the water, turned to face me, and drifted my way. The perfect gift for a boatman."

Serge paused, reflecting back, and then continued. "There was another message, written on yet another piece of parchment. Not the pouch. I found it in the tool bin and carried it with me into the vault, and it eventually became lost in the debris. That's why you didn't find it. The message described the corridor and said that the thousands of keys mounted on the walls and ceiling of the corridor are firmly attached—except one. It would take time to find the special key, but it could be lifted off its mount and carried away. The message said that the key is large, and that engraved on one side of the key is the sketch of a door—who knows where—that the key unlocks. The parchment also contained a drawing of this key, and drawn next to the key was a most beautiful door. Somewhere in this world, the door really exists. But it did not say where this door is located or where it leads. Next to the drawing of the door, the parchment also contained a profoundly beautiful painting of what can only be described as paradise. It was a paradise somehow connected with Earth. Somewhere on Earth, the door to paradise exists.

"Anyway, neither my body nor, later, my spirit form could get into the corridor to search for that key. But now I'm free. Thank you."

Then Serge waned, blended in with the windblown shadows, and disappeared from this world, leaving the word "paradise" ringing around the Rainbow Room.

"What exactly is paradise?" Chel asked. "Is it heaven?"

Grandpa hesitated. "Some would say so. But I think of paradise as a place like the Garden of Eden. Or a place of such extraordinary beauty and happiness that it is unimaginable. At least, this is the kind of paradise that Serge was describing—not heaven. If one has the key and knows where the entrance is, then one can visit paradise and return."

Evening was approaching, and there was silence while each of the four in the Rainbow Room reflected on what had taken place that day. "I am sure we'll have many conversations about this in the future," Grandpa said.

Chel smiled. "And I'm looking forward to that."

◊

By noontime the next day, the wind had subsided and the sky was clear. Grandpa was conversing with a friend who was driving him to the beach, three hours from home, so that Grandpa could retrieve his car.

Earlier he had phoned the Coast Guard near the beach to ask if anyone had found a boat adrift and, if not, to search for one. The receptionist transferred the call to the commander, who asked Grandpa if he was the owner of an abandoned boat named *The Vault's Keeper*, and if so, to please come to the station with its registration and other proof of ownership—and some photographs of the boat if he had any. The commander said that Coast Guard personnel were currently searching registration files. He also told Grandpa that within the past few hours, the Coast Guard had had an unusual experience with the boat, and that they had something for him.

The large white Coast Guard building was set prominently on well-maintained grassy acreage on the inner coastal waterway. Grandpa eased into the wide, neatly manicured U-shaped driveway. A large white sign with blue lettering, THE UNITED STATES COAST GUARD, greeted him from the center of the U.

Grandpa met with the commander and his assistant in a large bright office overlooking the wide sunny lawn and waterway. The commander explained that they had found the boat adrift that morning. There was no response when signaled, nor was there any sign of life on board. The commander wondered if the boat simply came loose from its moorings and drifted away. Grandpa offered no other explanation.

The commander began his explanation. "What happened was remarkable. As the crew of our Coast Guard cutter approached, they saw *The Vault's Keeper* inscribed on the boat. What happened next was . . . well, they had never seen anything like it. As they approached your boat, it turned to face them. Then they saw the stern begin to rise, even though the bow didn't go under. We have all this on film. The stern became . . . It was as if the boat were floating on the tip of its bow!"

Taking a deep breath, the commander continued. "Then the perpendicular boat just disappeared straight down into the ocean, without even a ripple."

Grandpa was stunned. He pondered the commander's description. It had vanished in a manner similar to which it had arrived—straight out of the depths, bow first.

"We found no floating aftermath to speak of . . . except for one thing," the commander declared. "We salvaged just one thing for you. The crew recovered a colorful softball-sized fishing float bobbing on the water."

The commander reached down into a drawer of his desk to retrieve the float, which was attached to a fishing line. As the commander lifted the float and line from the drawer, Grandpa finally saw the attached hook, and dangling from the hook, he saw the impressive prize: one especially large ornate ancient iron key, inlaid with abstract but beautiful designs of gold and silver. Engraved on one side of the key was a most beautiful door.

No one uttered a sound. All stared at the extraordinary key. It was about a foot long, including a large ringed handle on one end and an ornate complex lock piece on the other. Its gold and silver glimmered as it slowly rotated on the string. The commander was fascinated by it. He held the key up to the window and then to a shaded wall. No matter how he positioned it, it was undeniably the most beautiful ornamental device they had ever seen.

◊

Grandpa could barely keep his eyes off the key on the drive home, drawn to the etching of the door as described by Serge. Also, he pondered the central question: Where is the door that this key unlocks?

That morning, Grandma had phoned Exi and Chel to ask them to come over; she told them that Grandpa would have some news about the boat. They were anticipating this when Grandpa hiked into the house with key in hand

and eagerly joined them and Grandma to tell his story over a cup of coffee. "I couldn't believe it! I barely believed it when Serge talked about it. *This key!* Whatever is behind that door has to be something extraordinary."

"Extraordinary, indeed," Grandma remarked.

"You . . . you mean you know what's on the other side?" Grandpa whispered.

"Oh, no, no," Grandma answered. "I was just agreeing with you. This seems to be the key that Serge described—the one that would open the door to paradise. I would like to know, though, very much."

In the meantime, Exi and Chel were examining the key and were overcome by thoughts of mystery and beauty conveyed by the key. Chel responded, "We've just got to find the door!"

They pondered in silence for a moment. Finally, Grandma asked Grandpa and the girls to describe, step by step, their journey from the time they crawled into the vault until they spilled out onto the Rainbow Room floor. "And don't leave out one detail."

As Chel got to the point of describing their encounter with the ten extra large keys protruding from the wall and forming a stairway to the ceiling, Grandma's eyes began to widen.

As Exi was describing the superbly intricate and ornate golden door "inscribed" on the ceiling, she abruptly stopped, and simultaneously Chel gasped. The two girls looked at each other, mouths agape.

Grandma witnessed the exchange and turned to Grandpa. Looking him straight in the eyes, she said, "Aha!" She stood up and announced, "Follow me, you three, and bring the key! And also bring the key with the two circles—you know, the one that unlocked the last door on your journey."

The four adventurers then left the kitchen, trotted into the Rainbow Room, crawled in through the corner flowerpot cabinet, and went for a visit to paradise.

Turning Visible

Grandma was frantic. "Something's wrong with Grandpa!" she exclaimed to Exi and Chel as they entered her house for a visit. "He's slowly turning invisible!"

The two girls looked at each other in amazement and turned back again to Grandma. "That's impossible! What do you mean, Grandma?"

"Follow me. He's in the Rainbow Room."

"Hi, girls." Grandpa smiled as his two sweethearts walked into the Rainbow Room. "Don't panic. I'm not fading away. I'm just becoming a little more transparent."

Grandpa was reclined in his wicker rocker. They could actually begin to see the back of the rocker by looking straight through him.

"No time for your jokes!" Grandma asserted. "This is not funny. What are we going to do?"

"What happened?" Chel asked.

"Yeah, what happened?" echoed Exi.

"Girls, Grandpa sat down to relax with a glass of his favorite Porto. But he accidentally read the label backward. He grabbed the bottle of Otrop!"

"Whaaat?"

"Yes! He poured himself a glass of Otrop and drank it—by mistake. Then he called me and said that his hands were beginning to look kind of cellophane-like. That's how all this started. That was about an hour ago, and it has obviously progressed since then."

"What in the world is Otrop?" Chel immediately asked.

"It's a rare wood finish. It's made for magicians. They use it to finish wood props for magic shows. You polish wood with it, those wooden pieces that you want to blend in with the background so that the audience can't see them. Kind of like those lizards you can't see on trees unless you know they're there."

"And Grandpa drank Otrop?" Exi asked in disbelief.

Grandma read the label aloud. "The wood will slowly appear to blend in with its background. Within twenty-four hours of the time that Otrop is applied, you will not be able to see the polished wood at all. If you do not put enough polish on the wood, then the wood may still be seen to some extent."

"Grandpa, how do you feel? We're so worried that you—"

Grandma cut in. "Let's pray he didn't drink too much Otrop."

"Fine," Grandpa answered the girls. "Clear as a . . ."

"Stop it! You are *not* fine! You should be gravely worried!" Grandma finally dashed from the porch to call nine-one-one.

Grandpa winked at the girls. "She's afraid she won't be able to look at me anymore."

"Grandma's right, Grandpa. You are not funny," Chel announced.

"Anyway, I'm not fading away any more. I only had one glass of it. In fact, within the last few minutes the process has reversed itself, and slowly I'm becoming more visible!"

Exi picked up the Otrop bottle and continued reading the label aloud where Grandma had left off. "Caution: If you use *more than one teaspoon per two hundred pounds of wood*, then the wood will become oversaturated. In that case, the wood will start to become invisible as it is supposed to, but then the process will reverse itself and slowly the wood will begin to become visible again. However, this change will not stop. A churning will be observed. Within two to five minutes, the wood prop will begin to turn inside out; a once nice-looking prop will become an unattractive mess."

Chel exclaimed, "My God, one glass is much more than a teaspoon."

Exi nodded but noted, "But Grandpa is not made of wood. He's of flesh and bone."

They both shuddered in panic when they simultaneously realized that the pattern of changes that had been described for wood was, so far, being followed to a T by flesh and bone.

"We've got to save him!" Exi was frantic. "What can we *do*?" She stared at the bottle of Otrop. "Otrop, Porto" she pronounced, still staring, now seeing something else inscribed on the label. "Otrop derives its name from a patented method of reversing the complex process that producers of vintage Porto use to create their product."

She immediately passed the bottle to Chel and flew to the liquor cabinet, hurriedly shoving bottles around, grabbing the Porto and running back to Grandpa, popping open the bottle. "Grandpa!" she screamed. "Quick—open your mouth."

At the urgency in Exi's voice, Grandpa complied.

"Drink!" Exi ordered. She stuck the bottle in Grandpa's mouth and poured down his throat an amount she estimated to be as much as a full glass of wine, while Grandpa gagged and spewed some of the Porto on himself and Exi. She dumped some more down his throat, estimating the amount that was coughed up, making sure not to underestimate.

But this time Grandpa interrupted, grabbing the bottle. "What are you *doing*? You don't need to rush like that."

Meanwhile, Grandma had completed her nine-one-one call, and upon hearing the commotion, she rushed back to the Rainbow Room. Chel explained the scene as she and Exi were cleaning up the mess.

"Up to five minutes," Exi said. "Then we'll know if it worked."

Five minutes passed with no deterioration. Six minutes passed. Seven minutes. "He's okay," Exi announced.

Grandpa was slouched in his rocker, his shirt a wet mess, his eyes watery, a grin unfolding, a slumped arm grasping a half-empty bottle. "Okay. I guess I'm back to normal now."

The Detectives

Chel came screeching into the Rainbow Room. "Grandma! Grandpa's been arrested!"

Grandma lifted her head from her reading and simply looked at Exi over the rim of her glasses.

"It's true! I heard it on the radio—a special announcement! He's been arrested for armed bank robbery!"

"Calm down, Chel," Grandma said. "One thing Grandpa won't do is a stickup."

"He did it with a water pistol, and it worked . . . almost!"

Grandma gracefully rolled off her recliner. "Okay, Chel. Let's see what this is all about."

They went into the den, where Grandma flicked to the local news channel.

"A man is being held on charges of robbing a quarter of a million dollars from First Union Community Bank two hours ago," said the reporter. "Using a water pistol, the local magician flimflammed a bank teller into giving him the money. He left the bank only to be arrested a few minutes later when police were waiting for him near his home, after six independent witnesses at the bank recognized him and called the police. However, the stolen money has not been recovered."

Now Grandma became hysterical. She had heard serious siren activity nearby only two hours earlier.

◊

At police headquarters, Grandpa cried to Grandma, "I didn't *do* it."

The best part of Grandpa's day was seeing Grandma come into the holding cell to see him. The girls were too young to be allowed in the holding area, but they had written a note that Grandma was to give him.

"I left the shop as usual and was coming home as usual when all of a sudden all hell broke loose. I don't understand! *Guns* . . . the whole works! Now I'm here in jail cuffed to bars. *I didn't do it!* I didn't do anything wrong."

"Calm down, dear." Grandma asserted herself in the kind, private tone that registered with Grandpa. She reached for his hand, couldn't find either hand free, grasped the reality, and then touched his face.

Grandma knew Grandpa well and she tended to believe him, even though the preliminary reports had him dead-on. And he had a habit of doing strange things sometimes.

He read the note from Exi and Chel:

> We love you, Grandpa, and we know you didn't do it. We will help you find the real robber.
>
> Love,
> Exi and Chel

After only twenty-four hours in jail, Grandpa was released on bail. The police had neither the stolen money nor the fake weapon to keep him in jail; all they had was hearsay and a slightly blurred bank surveillance film, although when the police examined the film, they did note that the robber resembled Grandpa, but they could not make a positive ID. But none of the officers objected to the decision to release him; they figured he might lead them to the money.

When Grandpa arrived home, all he wanted to do was lie down and sleep, but he was too upset and confused for that. He wanted to be close to Grandma, and he always appreciated the warm attention from Exi and Chel.

Then the girls made their disclosure: "We have a message from Uni. Go to your shop and try to climb up to The Wonderful Place."

The shop was only a half mile from home. It was late in the day, but the sun was still up, so Grandpa decided to walk, figuring that since he couldn't rest, the exercise and fresh air might do him some good. Exi and Chel went with him. They took an obscure back way through the woods and the park to avoid any reaction from some police who were parked down the street.

They walked onto the driveway, which circled around the shop in horseshoe fashion and offered some parking places in back. Farther back from the shop stood the massive oak tree.

They marched up to the oak. Grandpa had planned to follow up on Uni's strange request. He approached the cavern to crawl through to the disguised stairwell door leading up to The Wonderful Place. But the cavern was blocked; it appeared that someone had stuffed it with leaves and branches. Exi and Chel removed them, only to find that they served as camouflage. Wedged in the space between the camouflage and the door was Grandpa's green duffel bag with his name sewn onto a label by Grandma when she gave it to him as a gift several years earlier. It was stuffed.

"I hope you're removing that thing!" The three startled humans turned around to see Uni standing behind them. "You asked me to come down once in a while to keep an eye on the shop, but then you stuffed up the cavity with a bag and leaves and stuff to make it difficult for me to do that. This space is too cramped for a unicorn as it is. This morning I had to struggle to get the bag and leaves out of my way to pass through, and not knowing the circumstances, I struggled to put this stuff back in place."

Grandpa turned to the girls and explained that over the past couple of months, strange things had been occurring at the shop. A few odd items were missing, including the duffel he used to take items to his shows. So he had asked Uni to occasionally pop in after store hours to check things out and to let him know if she saw anything suspicious.

He turned to Uni. "What do you mean by saying that I put the bag there?"

"I saw you do it yesterday. You were in such a rush I didn't want to bother you," Uni replied. "You were driving away from the shop just as I was climbing out of the tree. Then, no more than thirty seconds later, you came running back on foot and crammed the bag into the tree cavity, crammed some leaves and junk in front of it, and ran off. By then, I was standing in the shadows watching you."

"Chel, would you please run to the workshop and bring me the flashlight?" Grandpa requested.

Grandpa updated Uni about all that had transpired, and then he removed the bag from the tree and shined the light around the cavern to verify that it was empty. He also checked that the disguised interior door to the stairwell was closed—that the root-based cavern looked like the few others around the roots. He was confident that the thief, while knowing about the cavern, did not know about the door to the stairwell to The Wonderful Place.

"You mean, when you left to go home, you didn't immediately return with the bag?" Uni asked.

"That's right. At the time you thought you saw me rush back and cram the bag into the cavern, I was being arrested a few blocks down the street near the house."

"Someone who was impersonating you came here with the bag!" Chel quickly concluded.

"Yeah, and that someone is the bank robber," Exi added, unzipping the bag and peeking in. "And that someone is going to be coming back here for the money when the heat dies down, which is, like, any time now."

Uni quickly asked, "Who did it?"

"It's someone who knows me and my shop fairly well. Some of the stuff that was stolen from the shop was makeup and a wig made to look like my hair. The thief had to have been observing me long enough to know of the caverns in the tree, at least this large cavern . . ."

Grandpa suddenly froze, his eyes widened, and then he faced the girls. "I know who did it!" He paused to think, closing his eyes. "It's got to be him," he whispered to himself. "Who else?"

Then he faced the girls again. "His name is Raker. Remember two months ago when I gave a short course in my shop on the art of magical costumes and disguises? There were five students. Four I knew previously. They were customers with whom I've had long-standing associations. But the other student was a stranger and a loner. I could not develop a friendly or trusting relationship with him. It's got to be Raker."

"I have an idea," Chel said. "Let's wait here, and when he comes back for the money, we'll catch him. Like Exi said, it should be soon—when he thinks the heat's died down."

Exi saw how they could accomplish that. "There are four of us here, and one of us is an incredibly strong unicorn, so . . .

"Absolutely not," Commanded Grandpa. "No telling what he'll do. Too dangerous. This is a police matter."

Exi begged to differ. "But, Grandpa, if we call the cops and they come over and see you, or any of us for that matter, with the bag of money, and Raker does not come by, then it's curtains for you. We can't hide the bag again and pretend we know nothing; that's probably a crime too."

Grandpa put his hand to his chin. "Hmm, a little dilemma. Well, let's . . ."

"*Quiet!* Someone's walking up the sidewalk in our direction." Chel's young ears saved the day.

"Shh! I think he's coming up the driveway—toward us!" Exi added.

Chel and Exi hid behind some thick bushes pressing against the back wall of the shop, and Grandpa grabbed the bag, and he and Uni hid behind the giant oak.

Raker had just reached the giant oak when two huge unicorns galloped out from around both sides of it. Pinned to the ground with a hoof, without breath or a prayer, Raker looked up into the two enormous pairs of eyes firing down at him, and in an instant, he knew he was a failed thief.

The police arrived to find Grandpa standing tall, with one foot grounded and the other on Raker's chest. Chel and Exi were nearby, sitting on a stuffed green duffel bag worth a quarter of a million dollars.

Grandpa peered downward. "You were a good student, Raker, but you failed the ultimate test."

'MOLLY

School was out for the summer, and Exi, Chel, and their grandparents had traveled to the coast for a few days' vacation. On the morning of their first day, the two girls were relaxing and sunning in a secluded area of the beach. The beach and ocean were bright and serene. For over an hour, they listened to the waves, and the only other activity came from an occasional flock of pelicans. They had just witnessed a pelican dive straight down from a distance of about fifty yards above the water for its catch, and they were in the process of talking about that when Exi's phone rang—and the tranquility was over.

"Hello?" Exi inquired.

"Help me!" the other voice begged. "Would you two *pretty please* help me?"

Then the call disconnected, leaving Exi staring at the phone with raised eyebrows.

Chel was close enough that she could hear those words. "What was *that* all about?"

"I haven't the foggiest," Exi said. "Sounded like a girl around our ages, though. But I didn't recognize her voice."

Chel broke in. "Maybe it was all a hoax—maybe she's a prankster."

"I don't know. She sounded pretty serious to me. She did have my number . . . I mean, I doubt she just dialed it randomly. Oh, and she used the phrase 'you two'! Maybe she'll call back."

"You know what? We have her number. Let's be sure to save it." Chel was curious.

The day was hot, and the girls decided that now was a good time to take a break and go to the stand for a cold drink.

The stand was attached to a small restaurant surrounded by beach dunes, picnic tables, and a couple of outdoor showers. They picked a shaded table, flopped their beach belongings on it, and carefully placed full cups of sodas in front of where they chose to sit. Chel's phone rang.

"Please, please help me, Chel."

"*Whaaat*?" This spooked Chel. "Who *is* this?"

"You don't know me, but I know who you and Exi are."

Chel sat down in front of her soda, and Exi slid hers next to Chel's in order to hear the conversation.

The voice continued. "All I need is a *friend*. For months, I have been making phone calls at random, and every once in a while a girl who sounds about my age answers. I try to get these girls into a conversation, but when they find out that I want a friend, and to meet, most just hang up on me. *Please don't hang up on me.* A few did agree to meet me. But when they first saw me, they shrieked and quickly ran away."

The voice was sweet. Chel had calmed down a little and was becoming curious again. "Why did they do that?" she cautiously asked.

"Because I'm *so* ugly," the voice replied.

"What do you mean?" Chel glanced at Exi and shrugged her shoulders.

"I am *so* ugly that no one wants to be near me," the voice cried. "I just *need* a friend or two. I live alone. I do everything alone. Can you two and I meet?"

Chel evaded the question. "Where do you live?"

"I live in the woods. Not far from your Grandpa's shop. It's that forest that's behind the park—the park that's kinda between the shop and your grandparents' home."

The two nodded at each other in recognition.

The voice continued. "That's how I got your cell phone numbers. I found them at your grandpa's shop a few days ago."

Chel stayed focused on the forest. "How can any person live there? It's a jungle—so rough and thick. There's not even a path that goes in there."

"Well, that's where I live. Alone. Few people ever see me. There's a lot that's weird about me, other than being the *ugliest* thing *ever*. If we ever meet, I'll explain more about where I live. I don't have parents that I remember. Maybe I used to, but I can't remember. And I don't go to school, but I can read—and I do teach myself things. Maybe I did go to school for a while and then just got . . . lost . . . or came here from outer space or something. But I am smart, which makes up for my ugliness to a limited extent.

"Well, what do you do?" Exi asked. "I mean, do you have a job?"

"I don't need much money—but I make things like toys, art pieces, and practical furnishings from things I find in the forest. Then I sell them to a few stores or have them on consignment. And people do like them—they just don't like me. I wear a disguise now when I go to the stores. I'm so lonely. But I have so much to tell friends. And to learn from friends, if only I had some."

Suddenly, Exi was taken aback. Her mouth widely opened and she touched Chel to get her attention. She quickly mouthed, "Tell ya later." Exi had remembered a peculiar conversation she had overheard about a year ago—and really didn't understand—when she and Grandma were at the large craft store in town. She overheard a man, who could have been the manager, tell a patron who was admiring a beautiful intricate wreath that "the girl is very talented and makes beautiful stuff, but she looks like a chaos machine from outer space, so we have her come in through the back doors and send her out of here as soon as we can before she scares away customers. Lately she's been wearing a disguise, but she still looks weird."

Chel continued. "What's your name?"

The voice said, "That's ugly too."

"Well, what is it?"

After a pause: "Mollyboltrightstagrut."

"*What?*"

"Mollyboltrightstagrut."

"What part of that is your first name?"

"That is my only name."

"What is it, again?"

"Mollyboltrightstagrut."

Chel had to break it up into simpler syllables. "Molly-bolt-right-stag-rut. Is that right?"

"Yeah. Ugly, huh?"

"Can we call you Molly for short?"

"No. That's the name I came with, and I feel that I need to be called that. Can we meet, pretty please?"

Chel hesitated. "Well . . . I would have to talk with Exi about that." She paused and noticed Exi's contemplative expression. "Okay, I'll talk with her and call you back in a few minutes. We have your number."

"Please, *please* call back," Mollyboltrightstagrut said.

"Bye now," Chel said.

Exi and Chel simply stared in disbelief at each other. Finally, Exi said, "Oh, what the heck. It may be interesting. Let's call her back."

Mollyboltrightstagrut answered the phone on the first ring.

"Okay, we'll meet you," Chel said.

"Oh, that is truly, truly so *wonderful*. I'm *so* happy. Can't wait, can't wait, can't wait . . ."

"But you'll have to," Chel said. "We're at the beach and won't be back till next Thursday. Tell you what. We'll meet you on Friday in the park." Chel looked at Exi and received a nodding approval. "At the children's playground. One o'clock."

◊

Exi and Chel were waiting, sitting on swings, pleased that no children were there in case she really did scare people. This thought had occurred to them only upon their arrival at the park a few minutes earlier, but since the park was empty, they figured that they really didn't need to change the meeting location.

Suddenly, they heard a screech from the wild. They witnessed Mollyboltrightstagrut's blazing emergence from the forest. Her arms were flapping like the wings of a flying eagle, and her legs were seriously pumping; her knees rose to her chest. At every pump, she almost doubled over. Her head bobbed like a chicken's. At varying angles, she jigged forward to meet Exi and Chel, occasionally unleashing a wide sideways hop. Halfway to the girls, she abruptly executed a cartwheel, followed by an ice skater's spin, before she fell down and rolled the rest of the way. She jumped up in front of them and kept jumping for a few seconds. She stretched out her arms, and her hands rapidly twitched open and shut. She chirped, "Hug me!"

"Whoa!" The girls exclaimed in unison. They were now standing behind their swings and facing the most unusual appearing "person" that they would ever face.

The first thing that they noticed about her face was her incredibly large eyes. At first, the irises of her eyes were vibrating from side to side, almost with the speed of a plucked guitar string. Then they began swirling around like a tip of a fan blade, one rotating clockwise and the other counterclockwise. Her nose was wildly puffing out and sucking back in like the motion of a huffing blowfish. She was waving her ears as if they were her hands, evidently in a gesture that said hello. Her purple hair stood straight out, making her look like one of those cartoon characters who'd just plugged a finger into an electric outlet. Then there was her smile. It literally went from ear to ear, and the ends of her smile were rapidly flapping at her earlobes.

She began frantically running in place, looking upward again, and erratically flailing her arms. "Please don't run away!" she begged. "Oh, but the two of you are so beautiful. I wish, I wish!"

Chel spontaneously announced, "Mollyboltrightstagrut, you really *aren't* ugly—you're just extremely peculiar."

"What?" Molyboltrightstagrut instantly was motionless. "I'm not ugly? Did I hear that right? Oh!" She began hopping around in circles, looking up into the sky while thrusting her arms upward also.

Exi agreed with Chel. "You are just . . . unusual. Your appearance, that is. And your movements."

"My movements?" She clasped her hands and placed them under her chin. "Oh, I see. I'm just excited, but I will calm down. You did *not* run away and you did *not* call me ugly." She rapidly pumped up and down on her toes a few times, and then she stood still. She extended her right hand while shyly looking down. Exi and Chel extended theirs, and they shook hands.

"Tells us about yourself," Exi said. "Where do you come from?"

Mollyboltrightstagrut sat down on the ground facing Exi and Chel, who sat back down on the swings. "That's one of my problems," she said. "I am working on that." The two sisters were staring at her in bewilderment. Her eyeballs were now bobbing up and down, but as one went up, the other went down. "I think maybe from outer . . . I had to leave my . . . home. The first thing I *clearly* remember was waking up in this little house back there in the forest, about two years ago. Before that, I have very few memories. I'll tell you more about that when we become friends."

Exi interrupted. "Are you saying there is a house back in that jungle of crowded trees and brambles?"

"Yes. Two large rooms. One about the size of a large master bedroom and the other larger than most living rooms. A small house but neat. I like it. But there is something extremely extraordinary about it. I'm almost afraid to tell you because not only will you think I'm ugly, but you'll think I'm a liar as well."

"We already agreed that 'ugly' is not the right word. You're not ugly," Chel said. "So go on with your *lie*." Chel was joking now, and she gave a short laugh. Then she suddenly felt embarrassed for giving the appearance of being too familiar with someone so odd with whom she had just met, even though she was enjoying the conversation.

But to her surprise, both Exi and Molyboltrightstagrut gave a chuckle.

"Okay, I'll tell you about the house. But don't run away."

"We promise," Exi said, speaking for her sister as well.

"It's invisible."

"No way!" Chel exclaimed. "How can anything be invisible?"

"Do you mean disguised?" Exi asked.

"Invisible from the *outside*, if the windows and front door are closed. Not from the inside. Inside, I can see the walls and things. I can look out the windows. But from the outside, the house can't be seen. If a window or the door were open, then you could see that part of the inside from outside—and what a weird sight that is. The animals can't see it. But they know by adverse experience that it's there, and they stay away.

"I simply remember waking up in one of the rooms, the bedroom—I call the other room the 'everything room'—and not knowing where I was, nor where I came from. But over the past two years, my memory of the past has been returning. Except for me, there was not another thing in the house other than things that were attached. No furniture, no toiletries . . . although there is a small bathroom in the bedroom."

She paused for a moment, thinking, and then she continued. "Oh, right! No, nothing. Not even clothes. Later I made some clothes from leaves and acorns . . . thistles and such. I discovered that I needed clothes after I ventured a little farther out of the area for the first time one day and saw clothes on people. They saw me too and became frightened. That's when I learned the importance of being careful: how to hide and how to disguise myself. Another story. Again I'm getting ahead of . . ."

"So what did you do when you first woke up in this invisible house?" Chel asked.

"Okay, the first thing I did was just look around. I walked around, cautiously, in utter confusion. I studied the walls, the floors, the ceiling, and the corners. I looked through all the windows. I saw a small bright green yard surrounding the house, and beyond that, I saw trees, roots, branches, and thick bushes everywhere. I went to the door and eased it open, peeking out as I did so. I haven't a clue how in the world a beautiful yellow rose, not to mention the green yard, can grow in a place so dominated by such dense foliage. But there it was, welcoming me to this world.

"I carefully stepped outside and looked around. That's when I turned and realized I could not see the house. Instantly, I flailed around and immediately hit the door and dashed back to safety. But through a side window of the door, I stared for a while at the rose. I wish I were a rose."

"Tell us about the rooms," Exi requested.

"Well, as I've said, nice things are *attached* in the rooms—attached to the walls and floors and ceilings. There is a constant flow of fresh water from a small waterfall in the everything room. I can put a glass in it for cool water to drink. I can adjust the temperature and take a shower in it. I can turn it on and off. My water is supplied by a well, and my electricity is supplied by a generator outside in the back. There's beautiful music all around and controls on a wall for selections and volume. There is a built-in stove and refrigerator. A built-in TV and radio. Let's see . . . There are shelves, attractive walls, ceiling lights, curtains, blinds, a few cabinets. Modern, good quality. Now that I have made furniture, utensils, and stuff, it's comfortable there."

These descriptions spurred her to reflect back. "It was difficult at first. I didn't know much. I got my first meals from garbage cans. I knew I needed tools, and I kept my eyes open for them. I eventually scrounged some up, although my first creations for sale were made from vines and small branches, and my first tools for those were my hands and teeth—and sometimes some spit. At first, I mainly made baskets and wreaths, but later I made more sophisticated items."

Then she got back on track again. "Oh . . . the house . . . There is one extraordinary thing in my little house. But you'll have to see it to understand it."

"What is it?" Exi asked.

"It's a huge telescope. It's in the center of the everything room, and it extends through the cathedral ceiling to way beyond the treetops. At twice the height of the tallest tree, there are built-in mechanisms, so from the control panel, I can rotate it and aim it in any direction to see throughout the cosmos. You won't believe this, but I can extend the telescope so far out and bend it so much, all from the control panel, that I can view the depths of the cosmos from the other side of the world. But you'll have to look into it to fully appreciate its applications."

"What do you mean? What do you see?" Chel asked.

Mollyboltrightstagrut simply shrugged her shoulders. "You'll have to see for yourselves. Of course, I'll be there to explain certain things."

Exi and Chel looked at each other, and Exi said, "Well, it sounds interesting, but I don't know. I'll talk with Chel about it. And maybe with my parents and grandparents."

"I completely understand," Mollyboltrightstagrut said. "Just please don't tell anyone where my house is located."

Exi made an observation. "With all these years being around here, we've never seen a telescope rising above the trees."

"It's part of my little house. It's invisible from the outside."

Exi and Chel again glanced at each other as if to say, *This really can't be!* Yet at the same time, they realized that they were conversing with the most unusual life-form they could ever imagine.

Mollyboltrightstagrut jumped up with her hands folded under her chin and her ears waving. "Tomorrow," she said. "Please?" However, now her eyes were more focused. Exi and Chel smiled.

The three agreed to meet at the same time, but at the edge of the forest, farther from of the play area, in case children—or adults—were around. Exi and Chel watched in amazement as Mollyboltrightstagrut executed a series of cartwheels, rolling off to the forest.

◊

On their walk to their grandparents' home, Exi and Chel deliberated over whether or not to visit the house in the forest. Chel asked, "Exi, do you believe all that: that there is a house in there, number one, and number two, that it's invisible?"

"Well," Exi said, "she did come out of the forest, and she went back in there. And she knows a lot about it.

Yeah, I think she lives there. So she must have some kind of house."

"And what about that mysterious telescope?" Chel continued.

"Well, why would she make up bizarre stories if she is trying to make friends?" Exi countered. "Plus, she seems so sincere." Exi reflected on that for a few seconds. "I doubt it's a scam. What would anyone get from us—this week's allowance? *Ha!*"

"Yeah, I think she's sincere too. Actually, I kinda like her," Chel said.

"She sure is smart . . . and interesting," Exi added. "I wish we could . . ."

Chel intercepted Exi's thoughts. "Wish her into becoming normal."

They walked in silence for a minute. Then Chel turned to Exi. "Let's go!"

Exi gave her a smile. "We gotta be crazy."

◊

Mollyboltrightstagrut was there first, hiding behind some bushes at the forest's edge, only to pop out at the sight of Exi and Chel approaching. This time, her appearance was not so bizarre, though she rapidly raised and lowered her arms about ten times. Exi and

Chel slowed down, and Mollyboltrightstagrut ran right up to them. Exi and Chel reservedly exchanged simple cheek-to-cheek greetings with her. Then Exi and Chel gave her a friendly once-over.

"Hi, Molyboltrightstagrut," Exi said. Exi squinted. Something was a little different about her. Now Exi stared at her directly. "You look . . . well . . . not quite as *extreme*."

Chel agreed. "Yeah, and you don't have as many of those seriously odd twitches and such."

"Oh, don't I wish," Mollyboltrightstagrut said. "I really wouldn't know. I don't often look into a mirror. I guess I'm just calmer today. But I want to tell you something. I thought about our conversation, and I changed my mind about something that I said. Just call me Molly for short."

"Okay," Chel said. "That makes life a little simpler." They all smiled before turning to face the forest.

"Do you dare?" Molly asked.

"Yes!" chimed the other two.

This odd forest was an area where few had ever ventured. It was more like a jungle; it was dark and treacherous, crammed with low branches, raised roots, vines, briars, and other impediments. Exi and Chel had come prepared. They wore protective hats, safety glasses, long-sleeved shirts, gloves, work jeans, and hiking boots. In their backpacks, they carried a sufficient supply of bottled water and some insect repellant. Molly led the way, slithering among the brambles and trees like a lizard through a familiar maze, though a bit slower than usual. The other two followed closely behind. Exi and Chel were amazed by what they saw. Sometimes they needed to step over raised ground and roots, and duck under low branches. At one point, they heard what they thought was the hoot of an owl, and when they looked up, they saw a great diversity of dense foliage and only small sections of the big bright sky.

At one point, Chel called up to Molly. "You *are* going to lead us back out of this jungle, right?"

"Oh, I'll think about it," Molly joked. In an instant, she excitedly announced, "Of course I will!"

Upon hearing this brief exchange in the middle of a jungle, Exi surmised that this sounded like they were all becoming better acquainted, and she smiled.

After twenty minutes of rugged travel, they came to a small clearing that dramatically contrasted with the dense forest. They stopped. It looked like a brightly lit golf green with a beautiful yellow rose growing near its center. Oddly, there was no rose bush—just the rose. And Molly told them that it was always there.

"Now I want you two to walk over to the other side of the green and tell me what you see there," Molly commanded.

"No way!" Exi exclaimed. "And collide with something we can't see!"

"So you really *do* believe in the invisible house," Molly softly said with a happy smile.

"Yeah, guess we do." Exi and Chel gave each other a quick glance. Then they caught Molly's smile, and they both thought that it was nearly humanlike and sweet; it was not nearly as extreme as the ear-to-ear flitter that they'd witnessed the day before.

"Follow me closely," Molly said. "And stay to the left of the rose. The door is just to the left and behind the rose."

They filed toward the door. Exi and Chel felt some hesitation, but their anticipation for adventure took over. As soon as Molly passed by the rose, she stopped, extended her left arm, felt around a little, grasped something not visible, twisted it, and pushed with her arm while letting go of her grip. An awakening image emerged. It appeared at first as a long, thin vertical line, but it widened to three feet. They stared into the everything room at the giant telescope secured soundly into the floor and ascending upward through the high cathedral ceiling. They heard the most beautiful music: a combination of new wave, light classical, and spiritual—and a presentation of several instruments featuring the echoes of flutes, strings, a piano, and angelic-like soft hums. Yet there was something extra in those sounds that they could not identify—and they loved it. This was a warm, loving, and fascinating presentation of a home.

Molly stepped in and turned to faced Exi and Chel. "Welcome to my home," she said. Her eyeballs rolled around a little, but she soon realized that, blinked for a bit, and then became focused. "Come on in. I have prepared some cheese and crackers—and iced tea."

Exi and Chel sauntered in through the doorway, stood still, and looked around. Molly closed the door to ensure they remained invisible. The room was larger than they had imagined. The decor had been masterfully created by Molly's artistic hands. Looking to the right, they discovered the gentle downward flow of water, cradled by a rocky wall, dropping into a small clear pond. In front of the pond, not far from the telescope, they saw an attractive wood table about the size of a card table, but the top, sides, and legs were engraved with abstract images of planets, moons, and stars. Slid under the table was one chair. Then turning and looking to the left toward the far corner, they saw a small refrigerator and stove. Next to these was a short counter with four drawers, and mounted on the right side of the counter was a sink. A window was centered on the wall, directly behind the telescope. The remainder of the wall, on both sides of the window, featured two beautiful floral paintings.

"Your home is so beautiful," Chel remarked.

"Make yourselves comfortable," Molly said. "My bedroom is through that door." Molly pointed to the door centered in the left wall, several feet to the left of the refrigerator. The girls wandered in that direction to take a look. The bed was the main attraction. It was almost as large as a queen-size bed. Of course, Molly had made it. It featured four enormous posts and a large headboard, and like the table near the waterfall, it displayed intricate engravings of objects in the cosmos. The bed was a dark brown, and the engravings were inlaid with synthetic gold that Molly had obtained from the craft store. Another feature about the bedroom was on the wall opposite the headboard: a large bookcase packed with books. The girls, now curious, stepped over to examine the books. All were about the universe.

The bedroom was gorgeous, but there was one item normally found in bedrooms that was not found in this one: a wall mirror. (There was a tiny hand-held mirror hidden in a drawer.) Before they left the bedroom, they scanned it one last time to make sure they hadn't missed anything interesting, since there was so much of interest in Molly's house. That's when Exi noticed a cord hanging from the ceiling, to the left of the bed when facing it. Then she noticed the faint lines outlining an attic door. She pointed to it. "What's that?" she asked Molly, who was standing in the doorway.

"Oh, that's my bedroom attic," Molly replied. "Would you like to see it?"

As the girls were unfolding the ladder, Molly flipped a switch near the bedroom door to turn on the attic light. The two sisters carefully climbed up, crawled in, and stood up. Wondrous colorful paintings of objects in the cosmos were the first things that caught their eyes. They were spread out on two walls that were facing each other. However, the main feature of the attic was what was on the other two facing walls: two large bookcases containing hundreds of books. Exi and Chel were sure they knew their subject matter before they approached one of the cases. But when they got there, they saw that the books were deeper than just eloquent descriptions of the cosmos. There were books about the foundations and theories of the universe: mathematics and physics books. These included books about the theory of relativity, the sun, galaxies, cosmic geometry, time, dark matter, quasars, solar eclipses, string theory, ions, rupes, rings, blazers, and moon dogs, to list a few.

The center of the attic featured a beautiful coffee table and two small comfortable sofas, each facing a wall of art. And there was good lighting by which to read.

Exi and Chel were absorbed. After ten minutes of exploration, Molly called up to them. "Have a good read. I'll meet you down here for snacks when you're ready."

Once they were back downstairs in the everything room, Exi said, "Molly, I thought you said your house had two rooms."

"It does," Molly replied. "Two rooms and an attic. But . . . okay. There *are* three rooms."

"Why do you have so much about the universe and mathematics?" Chel asked.

"Well, I'm just inspired by what I see, and I'm always trying to better understand it."

Despite all the wonderful creations that adorned Molly's home, the telescope in the middle of the everything room remained its main feature. "Let's go to the table by the waterfall and snack on some cheese and crackers," Molly suggested. "Do you like iced tea? I'll just grab these two chairs. When we finish, we'll sit at the telescope, and I'll let each of you view some interesting things in the universe—well, especially one thing."

Sharp cheddar cheese on crackers and sweet iced tea hit the spot. The small talk centered on the moon, and imaginative speculation on what might exist on the other side. Taking her last sip of iced tea, Chel finally asked, "What is the one thing that is so interesting?"

Molly stood up. "Let me show you. Bring your chairs." She stepped over to the telescope, and Exi and Chel followed. "This is a very special telescope. There isn't another one like it on Earth. It can bring in anything in the universe that you want to view, and it can even focus on small details as a microscope can." She pointed to a viewing screen the size of a large TV. "This is where you will see anything and everything in the cosmos. Watch the screen and I will take you on a tour. I'm just going to conduct some operations using this control panel here . . . Okay. Now what do you see?"

"It's beautiful," Exi exclaimed.

"That's Saturn, up close, with her many moons and her wide bright ring of particles. Now watch this. I'm going to leave our galaxy, the Milky Way, and go farther out into the universe."

Exi and Chel viewed what looked like a thick disc of enraged fire, which had a small pitch-black spot at its center.

"That's a black hole," Molly explained, pointing to the black spot. "It's a point that is so dense that anything that comes near it literally gets sucked in and disappears. The gravity of that center point is so great that even light from its nearby sun travels to it and becomes, say, *activated* when it gets near the black hole, before it gets sucked in—that's the wide bright rim that you see. Our galaxy has a black hole—many galaxies do—but we are far, far from it, thank goodness."

The wide variety of fascinating entities and events in the seemingly infinite universe kept Exi and Chel spellbound for half an hour before Chel returned to the question she'd originally raised during the snack. "What is it that you find so especially interesting in the universe?"

"Are you ready for this?" Molly asked. She adjusted some controls on the keyboard. "There it is!"

"What's so special about that?" Chel asked, staring at something unrecognizable on the screen.

"That's *Earth*," Molly said.

"No way!" Exi exclaimed, laughing as if it were a joke.

"Oh, but it is Earth," Molly retorted. "Look here." She pointed to an area on the screen. "You can see that this is the Gulf of Mexico. And look here. This is Florida. And over here is the West Coast. And over here, you can recognize Long Island."

"It's too big—too tall—to be the United States," Exi said, studying the irregular land mass on the screen.

"This is not a map with colors and boundaries drawn in," Molly said. She drew an imaginary line with her finger across the screen and then tapped the region above where she drew the line. "This is Canada. Most of the states are below this." Similarly, she drew a line indicating the border with Mexico.

A long pause passed before Exi Spoke. "Can't be. We're on Earth—not looking at it from outer space."

"We're looking at a film, aren't we?" Chel asked. "You're tricking us, I know."

"I guess I'll just have to prove it." Molly had anticipated that proof would be required. She grasped a small lever that could be steered in any direction, and with this, she placed a tiny yellow dot on a certain location in the United States. Then, by pushing a button, she zoomed closer to the dot. The girls could see the land mass growing larger and the land's ocean boundaries disappearing. After a few seconds had passed, they saw trees. They recognized the green grass surrounding the invisible house—and the yellow rose. But they also saw the invisible house!

"Now, I want you two to keep an eye on the screen. I'm going outside for a few seconds. Even when I come back in, don't take your eyes off the screen."

Molly stood up and went outside. A few seconds later, she came back in and sat down near the girls at the control panel.

"We didn't see anything different," Exi said, still glued to the screen.

"Wait ten minutes. Have patience," Molly politely said. "I wanted you to look at the screen so you would see that nothing was there . . . yet. Then when you do see something, you will understand how slow the speed of light is."

Even just one minute is a long time while peering at a still screen and waiting with anticipation for something extraordinary to appear. But Molly was prepared. She had given each a cup of the most scrumptious sweet corn chowder. Suddenly, they saw the top of Molly's head coming out the door. She took two steps to the rose, and Exi and Chel saw each foot and leg swing forward, while the other leg swayed back. She turned around to face the house. Then she looked upward to Exi and Chel. She extended an arm toward them and gave an exaggerated wave of her hand with a huge smile. "Hi there," she said, and the two actually heard that! Then she blew them a kiss.

"My God!" Exi exclaimed.

"What a spectacular showing," Chel said. "But what's going on? And why did it take such a long time for the pictures, or images, to show up on the screen?"

"The speed of light," Molly answered. "We are so far away from Earth that any observations from Earth to here, all of which are carried by light, take a while. When we are in this house, we are actually on a different planet. As soon as we step out the door, we are on Earth. About hearing my voice, I have no clue. The speed of sound on Earth is much slower, and in the vacant regions of the cosmos, sound doesn't exist. Sound needs air to exist. But that's another matter.

"Another *planet*?" Exi was confused. "How can that be?"

Chel empathized with that sentiment, but then she became puzzled by another thought. "Wait a minute; we also saw the top of the house. But it's invisible, right?"

Molly kind of brushed the questions away and changed the subject. "Oh, I'll explain those things later. And no, I don't have cameras and stuff hidden in trees to accomplish all this. I'm trying to make friends, not trouble. Besides, while I'm good with crafts, and I know a lot about the universe, that type of technology is beyond me.

"But I *do* know who has that type of technology—specialized cameras, complex telescopes, and so on. And because I am trying to make friends, I do have to bring out the truth, in time, delicately. I know you two have experienced a lot here today. I'll walk you home—well, to the outer edge of the forest. Think about it. Come back tomorrow and I'll explain. I will explain everything to you. Please, pretty please." She winked twenty times in rapid succession with her right eye and again gave a huge beautiful smile. "Tomorrow, *please?*"

"Absolutely."

"A hug, please?"

"Absolutely."

◊

It seemed to Exi and Chel that over the brief time that they had known her, Molly was slowly losing some of her severe peculiarities—she was becoming more humanlike. Yet they had never considered her strictly nonhuman. After all, she was highly intelligent, well spoken, walked upright, and smiled. That's why they were shocked when they met her at the edge of the forest the next day. She still had many irregularities, but she appeared to resemble, to a degree, a human girl.

"What's *this?*" Exi asked excitedly. "Did you use makeup?"

"No, why?" Molly asked.

"Well, you sure look different," Exi stated. "You're changing—becoming more human looking, I mean . . ."

"*What?*" Molly replied, standing on her toes. "How's that possible? Well, you just like me more, that's all. I'll have to break my rule of not looking into mirrors to see what you're talking about."

"Okay, let's go." Chel smiled with anticipation, and again they turned and faced the forest.

They made their way to the invisible door next to the yellow rose by way of the same twists and turns of the day before. Once inside the house, Molly took off to her bedroom, leaving the other two standing in her wake. A few seconds later, they heard some ecstatic shrieking, and Molly accelerated back to the everything room by way of two cartwheels and a jump. Then she stood still and covered her mouth with her hands. "Oops!" she cried. "I shouldn't have . . . Oh, what's happening? I do appear a bit more humanlike!"

"Yes, over these past three days, we could see subtle changes," Exi said. "It seems like you are actually becoming kind of, well, almost *pretty*. I would guess that it's happening right before our eyes. The question is, what's causing this?"

Oh, but did she react to the word "pretty"—and with more self-restraint than demonstrated in previous reactions. She stood on her toes in her familiar pose of hands clasped under her chin and both widened eyes focused toward the cathedral ceiling. After a couple of seconds, she dropped her hands and focused on Exi and Chel.

Then she spoke. "Well, yesterday you said, and Chel agreed"—she paused for a breath—"that my appearance and eccentricities seemed less extreme, so I gave this some thought. Let's sit at our table here by the waterfall. I have some things to disclose to you. The time is right because now you will understand. Also, just recently, I've made some new observations that I need to share with you two. First I'll bring the snacks and iced tea."

"I smell corn chowder," Exi announced.

"I'll bring that too," the hostess replied with a wink.

"Oh, and in the meantime, use some of my books and study up on the universe," she said jokingly, skipping off to the kitchen area.

Chel and Exi looked at each other and then snuggled into their comfortable chairs at the table.

◊

"Let me begin by simply saying that there has been a genetic mix-up in the cosmos," Molly said laughingly. "I'm sorry; it's just that I'm in such a good mood today. I'll start over. Let me simply say that I don't have *all* the answers.

"Going back to the first day we had a conversation, when you were at the beach, do you remember me saying that maybe I came here from outer space or something? Well, there is no *something* about it. Of course, I couldn't get into that then, or we wouldn't be here now, but I *am* from outer space."

"Oh my God!" Chel exclaimed loudly, catapulting herself upward off her chair. Immediately, everyone became quiet at this display. But Exi and Chel believed it instantly. Their reactions were more of relief than of surprise. It explained so much. Chel, now a little embarrassed, followed up with a more reserved statement, slightly louder than a whisper, while sitting back down: "I knew that."

Now the focus was on Molly. "Okay," she said. "You recall from yesterday that whenever you are in my house, you are on another planet, but as soon as you walk out the door you are back on Earth, right? And that it took ten minutes for the kiss to arrive?"

The two nodded.

"Well, early on—and I know so much more now—I wanted to know where I was while in the house. I did some calculations. Light travels almost six trillion miles in a year. So if something is a thousand light years from us, then . . . Oh, never mind. Let me simply put it this way . . ."

"Thank you," Exi and Chel mouthed in relief.

"My home is not in another galaxy. It's not so far as all that. In fact, it's in our galaxy, the Milky Way. In fact, it's even in *this* solar system! Otherwise, you would have waited *years* before seeing me wave and blow you a kiss from Earth! The planet you are on is where I came from."

"Oh, wow!" Chel said. "I don't . . ."

"The sun is the center of our solar system. Mars is the next planet farther out from Earth, and Jupiter is the next one farther out after Mars. But the kicker is that when Earth and Mars are in their closest proximity to each other, by way of their orbits, it takes approximately *five and a half minutes* for an image of Mars to reach Earth. It's similar with Jupiter. Jupiter is farther away, but at its closest proximity to Earth, it takes almost *forty-four minutes* for an image from Jupiter to reach Earth. So if you are peering upward to Jupiter in that near location in the night sky, the image you see is Jupiter, *historically*—not now—but forty-four minutes ago. "Are you following?"

Thinking heads were bobbing.

"An image of this planet requires ten minutes to arrive, as you saw yesterday when my kiss took ten minutes to get to you. Moreover, it *always* requires ten minutes for an image to go from the planet to Earth, and from Earth to there."

"Oh, this is getting complicated," Exi announced.

Molly recognized this and quickly responded. "I'm sorry. I'll try to keep it simple. So, simplifying a little, my planet is positioned between Mars and Jupiter. It is always the same distance from Earth, as if it's following

Earth. And it's a little farther out, so a little faster. Same size as Earth. Earth's shadow? No. Much older than Earth. Simple enough?"

"Yeah, I guess," Exi said. "But I have a question that's been nagging me. How can we be on a planet that is that far away from Earth, and at the same time simply walk out the front door and be on Earth?"

"It seems like a paradox, doesn't it?" Molly responded. "And there is more to it than that. I don't know all the technical details, but it has to do with the inhabitants of the planet. In a few minutes, when I describe these inhabitants, you will gain some insight into this.

Molly continued her dialogue. "The thing is, no astrophysicist, no scientist of any kind—no *human*—has ever detected this planet. *Until me.* It's not visible from Earth. I didn't know why for a long time. It's not in Earth's shadow like the moon is sometimes, and it's not a black hole that adsorbs light. The scientists there have figured out a way not to be seen by earthlings. Moreover, it can't be discovered using other equipment designed for detecting land mass and such. It can't even be seen by astronauts traveling near it. And for various reasons, it can't be hit by anything traveling toward it . . . but let's go to the telescope so I can show you the invisible planet."

"What?" Exi asked. "You just told us that the planet was invisible?"

"It is, to earthlings on Earth. But don't forget that you're not on Earth; you are on my planet. I know, I know, it breaks fundamental laws of geometry and physics. If you are in a house and the house is on Earth, you would think that you would be on Earth—not off on some faraway planet. But the inhabitants have many advanced geometries that they work with. It's a radically different environment there. You two can see Earth because you are looking at it from a faraway planet using a super telescope, and we can see the invisible planet using reverse telescopy because we are on it."

Exi and Chel were not going to get near that one—at least not at this time.

"Is that why you know so much about the planet?" Chel asked.

"I've been studying the planet for about two years. Not a day goes by without at least peeking in. It's the only planet with advanced life near our immediate part of the Milky Way, although there is life around other suns in the Milky Way . . . and in other galaxies."

Molly did some figuring at the attached electronic three-dimensional curved coordinate system, and then she positioned the small yellow dot and pushed the button to bring it closer to the planet at which she was aiming. A tiny ball appeared, and then it grew to the size of the screen. "That's it: the invisible planet," she announced. And what a sight it was. It looked like a symbol of love. It appeared as a circle with a perfectly shaped large deep blue heart in its center, surrounded by yellow. "The blue is one of the oceans, and the yellow is the land," she explained.

"Could we move closer? I would like to see what's on the land," Chel said.

"That will be another time, after I've explained some things to you," Molly said. "By the way, this is why you could see the house through the telescope, Chel, when you and Exi were telescoping me when I was standing out by the rose. Through the telescope, the house was visible because you were looking at it, not from Earth but from another planet. The house is invisible to earthlings on Earth, as I've explained.

"Now I must tell you what this is all about. As my memory of the past has improved, I remembered my 'people' telling me about Earth, and where it is, and where we were. They were preparing me for the trip to Earth. This planet is named 'Friend.' My people, the 'friendlings,' sent me here from Friend."

"Why would they do that?" Chel asked.

Molly continued. "Not for ill-spirited reasons—they are a kind and loving people—but to see if it would help me improve my looks. My people are *very* advanced—technologically, intellectually, culturally, scientifically . . . you name it. We have existed more than five billion years longer than earthlings have, so we have had that much more advancement. In fact, we existed five billion years before the sun and the solar system existed. Ten billion years ago, the friendlings moved the planet here because their original solar system was on the verge of collapse. The friendlings' super intellectual abilities and scientific advancement permits them to develop the technology to do these seemingly paradoxical things. The moment there is peace on Earth, Friend will become visible, and the friendlings will join the earthlings as partners in the continuous quest for intragalactic understanding and universal peace." Molly paused, letting Exi and Chel exchange incredulous looks.

"How . . . advanced . . . are they?" Exi was almost afraid to ask.

"Let me explain by giving you a comparison. It involves the flying disk that hovered over Chicago's O'Hare Airport in 2007 and was seen by many credible people, including pilots, service people, and passengers. After twenty minutes, the craft took off upward with an incredible acceleration and put a hole in a large thick cloud so that the observers could see the blue sky beyond the cloud. Yet radar and other surveillance equipment did not detect it. Whatever beings created this craft were advanced enough to be able to make the craft invisible to cameras and radar, but they were not advanced enough to make it invisible to the more biologically complex human eye. The friendlings are more advanced; they made Friend invisible to the human eye—and they made my house invisible too."

Chel needed more information about her initial curiosity. "How in the world would coming to Earth help you to improve your looks?"

"They sent me here because I was so vastly different-looking that it was causing problems with many friendlings. These wonderful 'people' are *very* different in appearance from earthlings. They're about the same size as humans, but their features are much different. Their heads are round, about the size of a basketball, with three circular eyes. Light always beams out of their eyes. Their mouths are thin but long; they are so wide that they extend out *beyond* their faces. A string of twenty or so bottom teeth protrude outward and are always visible. When they smile, the ends of their mouths bend downward. Their necks are thick and short, with Adam's apples that stick way out and are shaped like thorns, followed immediately by shoulders that droop drastically down. Their arms are about half the size of human arms, and each hand has only four fingers. Their chests and stomachs are shaped like two-drawer file cabinets. And they don't have knees, so their gait is odd by human standards. Ten toes on each foot. That lists just a few of the differences. Of course, they see each other as normal. They are great beings, just . . . different-looking. And I scare them. So when they look at me it's as if—okay—you two humans suddenly saw a dust mite the same size as you. Or a silverfish, or a bacterium, or a black widow spider, or a rattlesnake—except your size. Not just a wacky, spiraled-out almost girl. Know what I mean?"

Thinking heads were still bobbing. "Oh yeah—now that is *really* ugly," one head said.

"My approaching another friendling produces the same reaction as you would experience if a rhinoceros with open-mouthed dinosaur fangs approached you. So the friendlings had to do something."

"But, Molly, you still haven't answered my question about coming to Earth," Chel remarked.

"I'm getting to that. The friendlings concluded that out of all the advanced life-forms that they know of, humans are the closet to resembling ugly me. Now listen very carefully with open minds to what I have to say next. There is much more variety, or variability, or differences—I'm trying to find the best word. *Huge differences* will do—in appearances among the folks in Friend. Friendlings can change and improve their appearances under certain circumstances—within limits. It's odd. If one is considered not good-looking—or even *ugly*—by another, and the other loves or likes the personality of the ugly one, then the ugly one will notice an improvement in his or her appearance. The reason for this, and I think it's because of the advanced state among the friendlings, is that *character* comes first. Physical appearance is secondary. Generally, it's the opposite here on Earth. Oops, I mean *there* on Earth."

Molly caught the quizzical looks the girls gave her and said, "Sorry—simple, simple!"

"Character comes before appearance in attraction? Sorry, Molly, I don't understand." Exi felt a strong need to understand this.

"Okay, let me explain it this way. On Earth, personal appearance is the first thing in general attraction—character comes later. And the character of a person is often blinded by the attraction. On Friend, character comes first in love and in friendship. Love and friendship are based on character, and looks are secondary . . ."

Exi interrupted. "So . . . do you mean that on Friend, appearance is not nearly as noticed as character when one is getting to know another? Let me see . . . If, say, Bill is attracted to Ann because of her good character, and Ann isn't good-looking, then Ann's appearance will improve. Is that what you mean?"

Molly smiled. "Oh, you and your sister are so bright—you ask such great questions. Yes, that is a good way of putting it. Ann's appearance will improve up to the level of her character.

"On Earth, one may wish a person's character to change after the physical attraction for that person takes hold—but good luck. On Friend, it's the opposite; one may want the physical *appearance* to change after the love or friendship with a desirable *character* or personality is developing. And that is much easier. It comes about by the wishing, or the hoping, by the one who is attracted to the ugly one's character. This came about as part of our evolutionary process over the past ten billion years. Simple enough?"

"Yes," the girls answered hesitantly.

Chel added, "Character or personality, the second stage on Earth, can't change, but appearance, the second stage on Friend, can change."

"That's right," Molly said. "Look at it this way. Suppose you had a friend, a girl, and one of the reasons that you liked her was due to certain aspects of her character or personality, in addition to common interests and so on. But suppose she was ugly and wished that she were attractive. Further, suppose you had a way to make that happen, say, by a superior ability of *wishing*. Wouldn't you do that for her?"

"Oh, yes!"

"Okay, good. But like all things, as I alluded to, there *are* a couple of limitations. The first is, and I mentioned this a minute ago, that your physical beauty can develop only to the extent of your inner beauty—of your character. Even though we are advanced, we are still only friendlings. The other limitation is this: if one is *extremely* ugly enough to cause fear as I do to them—as a two-hundred-pound spider with fangs would be to most humans—then the progression toward beauty won't happen."

Molly paused, and Chel took over. "So they sent you to Earth with the idea that you would not appear so extremely ugly to humans so as to cause fear, because you looked kinda humanlike. Then some humans might like your character and become friends, and then, as your new friends would wish, you would gradually become prettier from a human perspective—and have a happy life as a human, as Exi and I hope."

"Exactly," Molly said with a tear in each beautiful eye. "As I said earlier, there is something else that I just figured out in the last day or so. I feel my features changing as I pass by the yellow rose. And the more we get to know one another, and become friends, and hug, the more I feel the changes when I walk by the rose. And I think the rose has some effect even when I'm in the house. I never knew the purpose of its existence. The friendlings must have planted it here when they built my house. Let's step out the door to Earth and be by the rose."

The three went outside, onto the sun-brightened green grass. Molly looked down at the rose, and then she looked up, and with both hands, she wildly blew a kiss into the sky. She felt the kiss returned, one on each cheek . . . and then she realized that Exi and Chel had given them to her.

"Molly, you are *beautiful!*" Chel declared.

Exi agreed. "You have the grace of an angel."

"It was the hugs, friendship, the best wishes, the good character, and the magic of the yellow rose," Molly said.

Exi and Chel were stirred. They looked at each other, and in the presence of Molly's smile, they embraced in a huge hug. And when they parted, each holding both hands of the other and bending slightly back for a good look at the other—a pose sometimes observed in reunions of long-parted friends—each noted that her sister was a bit more beautiful than before.

THE TENANT

The sign boldly called down from the front door of the magic shop to the street: ROOM FOR RENT. A sinister-looking figure was moving from the street to the door.

Grandma saw him coming.

He was dressed in dark clothing, and his face was hidden deeply inside a huge dark gray hood. He walked as if gliding, his cloak evoking thoughts of wings. His hood was angling from right to left as he flowed forward, as if to warn the moths to keep back. He was a giant.

Grandma was in the front area of the store. She was in charge of screening potential roomers for the vacant attic room in the store. But in watching his approach, she had nothing but negative feelings about the stranger.

"The rent is high here," Grandma offered, backing away as the hooded giant bent down to enter the store. "The rent is . . ."

"I am not here to rent," the awful giant interrupted. "I'm here to see Exi and Chel."

Grandma nearly collapsed at the thought.

The hooded giant swiftly walked past Grandma and through the doorway to the backroom workshop, where Grandpa and the two girls were working on a new magic trick. He closed the door behind him.

Grandma took a deep breath, tiptoed to the workshop door, and listened in. She heard nothing. Then she walked in.

Grandpa and the girls were working on their project. "Hi, Grandma," the girls said.

"Any good prospects for a tenant yet?" Grandpa asked, focusing downward at nothing.

"Where'd he go?" Grandma demanded.

"Where'd who go, Grandma?" Exi returned.

"The tall hooded creature that just came through this door, *that's who!*" Grandma exclaimed.

Grandpa and the girls looked at each other, and then they looked back toward Grandma. They all appeared unconcerned.

"A tall hooded creature?" Chel queried.

"Yes! Don't tell me I'm seeing things. He walked right past me and into this room."

Silence.

Grandma felt that the three of them might as well have been winking at each other. She noticed part of an empty dark gray hood on the floor, spilling out from behind a cabinet near the back door.

She mulled over all of this for a second. Then she turned and briskly walked back into the front of the store, feeling as though she had been the victim of a trick played by loved ones. She felt betrayed, hurt.

Forty minutes later, Grandpa and the girls paraded into the front store area to tell Grandma about their new successful stunt involving a tall hooded creature. Instead, a regular and trusted customer was standing there by herself.

Grandpa glanced around. "Oh, hi, Joan! Where's Lyn?"

"Oh! Hi. Well, I don't know now," Joan said. "We were both here not more than a minute ago, when this freaky-looking giant hooded . . . creature . . . appeared at the door. Lyn smiled and assured me that it was only a joke. She said it was the girls and you stacked on each others' shoulders and buried in a cloak. So you three offered an arm, and off you went. But now you and the girls are here!"

"Oh God, where'd they go?" Grandpa was horrified.

"I thought it was you and the girls," Joan became apologetic. "They mentioned something about the fairgrounds, which seemed to please her. She asked me to look after the store for a while."

The three raced to the fairgrounds. Grandpa knew well the world of human magic. But he also believed in the existence of supernatural magic, which could reach beyond the real and ordered world, becoming an independent source of evil. But he had never experienced that, until now.

Rushing onto the fairgrounds, they saw, in the distance, the tall hooded figure pulling a resistant woman. She was waving in distress. The giant was dragging Grandma into the house of mirrors.

The three rushed through the entrance of the house of mirrors to find themselves faced with several mirrored corridors forming a maze.

They ran through one corridor and came to a large room whose curved mirrors created such a disorientating effect that they had to stop. On the far side, they saw the giant and Grandma take one step toward them and then vanish.

The three rushed to that location but found nothing. They looked around and saw the giant walking backward and simultaneously walking forward, as if doing the moonwalk. Grandma was stumbling trying to keep her balance, reaching out for Grandpa with her free arm.

She was looking back and forth in desperation between Grandpa and whatever direction she was headed. The scene was frenzied, but her face was frozen in fear. The giant's hood was oriented toward Grandpa, who felt a sinister expression reaching out from within its hollows, taunting him. Then they simply disappeared again.

In the next instant, the unnatural pair was multiplied by the confusion of mirrors, seen everywhere at once, moving quickly in all directions. They flew over the three and then vanished. Suddenly, the hall of mirrors was still and silent.

"They're gone!"

"We have to get out of here!"

"Yes! Look for an exit sign."

They exited through a back door onto the fairgrounds. "Look!" Exi screamed. "Over there." Exi pointed to a 1950s-era drugstore complete with signs that advertised fountain sodas, milkshakes, and egg creams. The giant was standing in the front door, beckoning the three to come into the drugstore. Having been noticed, he glided backward into the drugstore, bowing down to fit through the door, one arm holding Grandma, one arm presenting an invitation to follow.

Grandpa and the girls raced to the store and found it almost empty. Seated across the way were two boys, and that was all.

"Hey, that's Steve and Tom," Chel pointed out, reminding Grandpa that brothers Steve and Tom were the high school gymnastic champions who lived next door to Grandma and Grandpa.

"Have you seen a tall hooded fellow with Grandma in here?" Grandpa asked, wasting no time.

Tom looked straight at Grandpa. "Yes. We are he!"

The brothers pointed to one of two piles of items on the floor against a wall. In that pile, Grandpa saw a dark hood and a crumpled horse-sized cape.

Grandpa took a few seconds to unravel his thoughts. "Where's Grandma? Is she all right?"

"Yeah, she's fine. She's a bundle of laughs, as always," Steve said.

"She had to go to your store to make some last-minute arrangements for the new tenant," Tom further explained.

"New tenant? What new tenant?" Grandpa asked. "What are you talking about?"

The boys pointed to the second pile on the floor, where Grandpa saw his biker boots standing on the floor next to a pile of his jeans and shirts, on top of which he recognized his blood pressure medications and his toiletries. And propped up front against this stuff was the book he had recently read. Its large cover title reached out to Grandpa: *Two Can Play the Game.*

As confused Grandpa and the four youngsters were leaving the old drugstore to head for his new apartment, Grandma met the group just outside the door. "Boys," she exclaimed, looking at Steve and Tom, "would you take those two bundles to the house, please? Grandpa and I will fall in behind you."

Grandma turned to the girls. "You two go to the shop and help Joan. And tear down the ROOM FOR RENT sign. Grandpa and I are going home for a little discussion. Oh, and Exi, Chel, think about whether you've learned anything today!"

Grandma and the embarrassed, tricked magician—with his tail dragging behind him—turned and went home.

THE IMPORTANCE OF HITTING THE TARGET

Grandpa suddenly awoke in the backyard, standing, back up against the house. His mouth was stretched with fear. He was facing a monster.

The monster was insect-like, with wings arching upward like prayer hands over its head. The wings were lit by whorls of disco bright yellows and hues of blues. Grandpa saw eyes like those portrayed in movies about outer space aliens, dark and bugged, and what looked like tractor components churning on its lower face. Its face was pushed up to Grandpa's, eye-to-eye.

The monster was not attacking Grandpa; rather, it was guarded, displaying extraordinarily quick and oddly angled contortions. It studied Grandpa up and down.

The fact was that Grandpa had invaded the monster's space. The space where Grandpa awoke had been empty until, within a billionth of a second, he spontaneously appeared in the face of this creature. Grandpa had been on his recliner in the Rainbow Room for his early afternoon nap when instantly he found himself in this predicament.

But Grandpa's troubles deepened. Glancing above the monster, he saw yet other threats. A giant humanlike form was swiftly moving toward him. He instinctively raised an arm to shield against what appeared to be a giant, round spiderweb raging down on him. Grandpa's knees began to buckle.

"Grandpa!" Chel screamed, discontinuing the motion of her butterfly net, which was extending downward to catch the butterfly that was in Grandpa's face. "Oh my God!"

Grandpa now recognized Chel's face as that of the approaching humanlike form, and her net as the aggressive web. But Chel was a *giant*!

"Grandpa! Is that you? Grandpa! That's you, right? Grandpa! You are so *tiny*!" Chel froze, awaiting a response.

Grandpa was now simply flopped on his rear, his arms and hands extending behind him to the ground, propping him up, and his mouth was open to the sky.

"Chel, thank God for you! You saved my life."

"No, I didn't. I accidentally almost took it."

"But, Chel, I . . ." Grandpa's voice faded, but he managed to continue. "What is happening to . . . ? I don't underst—"

"Grandpa, *listen*," Chel interrupted, nestling down on her knees in front of Grandpa. "I was looking for butterflies, and I saw this one and came over with my net to catch it. Suddenly there you were!"

Chel paused. "I know you do weird things sometimes, Grandpa, but what's all *this* about? You're an inch tall!"

The butterfly had fluttered away by now, but she was still within listening distance.

"Chel, the last thing I was doing before appearing here was napping. I don't know what happened. Occasionally, during my naptime, I perform astral projection. I . . ."

"Astral *what?* Please make sense, Grandpa."

Grandpa was regaining his composure and beginning to understand at least some of the gravity of his present situation. "I'll have to explain. It . . . it must be related. I can't have Grandma or anyone see me like this." He paused and then continued. "Astral projection is an ancient but not well-known activity. After months or even years of practice, some people can do it."

"Astral projection!" Chel had to pronounce the term. "I need to know more to be able to help you."

"It's like this. You find a time when you will not be interrupted. You lie down on a bed or recline in some other comfortable position. Then you close your eyes and relax. You concentrate on relaxation. You hypnotize yourself. Self-hypnosis is the foundation of astral projection. The idea is to extract yourself from any and all physical sensations. Only your consciousness, without sense of your physical body, is present. Then you—your consciousness—can lift out of your body; you can look back and see your body lying there, eyes closed." Grandpa paused. "This is slightly simplified, but it's the basics. Okay?"

Chel was absorbed in trying to understand. "Will you explain how all this ties in with your tiny self?"

"I must," said Grandpa. "At this stage of concentration, and all this does take much concentration, because concentration is the—"

"Grandpa!" Chel interrupted again. "Skip the fundamentals and get on with what happened."

"I told myself to rise up out of my body and go into the den. I lifted out of my body and looked back down at myself stretched out in my recliner, comfortably sleeping. This is sometimes called an out-of-body experience."

Grandpa took a breath. "But next is the tricky part. Only the masters have total control as to where their consciousness will project. I somehow bypassed the den and arrived out here. I don't yet have good control of exactly where I land."

"Let me see if I understand. You can get out of your body. Your spirit or the conscious part of you—whatever—leaves your body. Is that right?"

"Good enough for now."

"But when you move in this spirit-like form, you can't control where you are going?"

"Unfortunately, I haven't been able to master that part yet. I am working on it, but I simply cannot hit my target."

But Chel realized that this situation was different from the astral projection that Grandpa described. "But it's not only your consciousness out here. You can't see consciousness," Chel speculated aloud. "It's the *total* you, just smaller."

"And that's what has me terrified!" Grandpa asserted. "That's never happened before, and I have never heard or read of this happening to anyone—that is, an actual physical transference." He paused, thinking. Then he made a request. "Chel, do me a favor and run to the Rainbow Room to see if I'm there, on the recliner."

Grandpa hid under a leaf, and Chel took off.

◊

"She won't find you there." The voice near Grandpa startled him, as if he had not had enough trauma for the day. But the day had only begun.

"Who said that?" Grandpa snapped as he as he pushed the leaf aside and turned to face the voice.

"I did," the butterfly said, being careful not to occupy Grandpa's space.

"I'm sorry, but I can't help being involved. My name is Flutter, and I'm friendly. I can help you."

"Whoa. What? You . . . can help me?"

"Yes. At least I can explain some things that should be helpful to you in your current state."

Grandpa nodded eagerly.

Flutter continued. "What you experienced is not astral projection. Actually, it's called 'astral transplantation,' which is different from astral projection."

But there was no time to explain. Chel came busting out through the back door. "Grandpa, you're not there! You're only here . . . and tiny. Ohhh! Grandpa, what are we going to do?"

Grandpa loudly said, "Chel, careful where you step!"

Chel knelt and bent over in order to hear.

"Calm down. Let me introduce you to Flutter. Chel, this is Flutter. Flutter this is Chel, my granddaughter." Grandpa nodded back and forth to each.

"Oh no, this is really serious. It's affecting your mind," Chel said, trying to get closer to comfort her little grandfather.

"Oh, I'm real!" Flutter interjected. Chel quickly straightened up, shocked at hearing the butterfly speak.

"Chel, I have a lot to say," Flutter continued in a serious tone. I am here on a special mission, which I will explain to you later because it concerns you. But for right now, the urgent mission is to help Grandpa."

Chel was all ears.

"I know a little about you and your family. I have seen you in The Wonderful Place at times when you visit. That's where I live. I know your friend Uni, who is the guardian of the portal at the base of the lollipop tree through which you enter The Wonderful Place from Earth when you come to visit. I come to Earth occasionally for special missions. That's my job. I'm a messenger."

Chel was a smart and curious girl, and in order to understand all that she could, she had to ask Flutter a burning question. "How did you get here? You're too small to open the hidden door on the oak tree, even if you get into the tree from . . ."

"You're right," Flutter said. "I have a quicker and more efficient way. But it is a *secret* way that is unknown even to the unicorns and the kangaroos. No human knows about it either. Only we butterflies know about it."

Flutter paused with a touch of sadness. "But now I have to reveal this secret to you and Grandpa. Even if I don't, you're going to figure it out anyway. I ask you both to honor the secret of the butterflies and never speak of this secret unless it's a matter of grave importance, which, as you will understand, is the case here. For your honor, you will benefit from the Society of Butterflies in The Wonderful Place."

Grandpa looked up to Chel. "Do you understand the importance of this?"

"Yes," Chel responded. "Do you?"

"Yes."

Both promised not to reveal the secret of the butterflies.

Flutter explained. "The best way of traveling to Earth and back to The Wonderful Place is by astral *transplantation.* This is different from astral *projection.* I will explain all this."

Chel and Grandpa were intensely focused.

Flutter revealed more about the nature of astral transplantation. "We butterflies are much larger in The Wonderful Place. Oh, you've seen us there. With our wings spread out, we are about the size of your bedsheets, but we are still not quite strong enough to open the doors in the tree that connects Earth and The Wonderful Place. But we have compensated by developing astral transplantation. Many of us occasionally visit Earth. We have butterfly friends and relatives who live on Earth. We are the only species in The Wonderful Place that has relatives in both places."

Flutter paused and then added, "Not all butterflies can perform astral transplantation. A few butterflies do it well. I am very good at it, which is why I have this coveted job as a messenger."

Flutter then looked at Chel. "This brings me to my mission, Chel, which is a message that we butterflies in The Wonderful Place wish me to give to you. This is why I came here today to Grandpa's house. I figured you would be visiting Grandma and Grandpa. The message is brief, and then we will get on with helping Grandpa."

"Okay," Chel agreed.

"We want you to please stop catching butterflies as a hobby."

This caught Chel by surprise. "But I just admire them and then let them go. I love butterflies."

"I know you love butterflies, and we love you back. But we're horrified by the prospect of being caught in nets. Besides, we could get hurt. Thank you for listening, Chel. Now let's get back to Grandpa's situation."

Chel's fallen expression was all that Flutter needed to see. Chel softly cried at the thought that she could be unknowingly hurtful.

Flutter turned to Grandpa. "The large you is the usual you. The small you is the transplanted you. How you did astral transplantation and got your small self here, I don't know. Only your consciousness should have been projected here. Humans have never done astral transplantation before, only astral projection. And the few humans who do the projection aren't very good at it. But as for the next step, transportation, that's beyond human capabilities. Perhaps you and I landing here at the same time caused something to get mixed up and caused you to become small, as I became small, but as I was supposed to.

She paused before adding, "Or perhaps you are just totally different from all other humans."

Chel smiled now.

Flutter continued. "When I prepare to leave Earth to go back to The Wonderful Place, I relax and hypnotize myself and do all the things you described to Chel earlier. I focus on the precise location at home from where I left. That's the spot where I will arrive as my large self. If my mind wanders and I focus on any other location for even a moment, or get distracted, it won't work. So that's what you need to do. The only way to become your usual large self is to hypnotize yourself. Target your recliner in the Rainbow Room and transplant yourself directly there. You must *concentrate*."

"Oh. Oh dear. Trouble ahead," Grandpa muttered.

Flutter interjected forcefully, "No. Think positively. Absolutely positively. And another thing: we need to transport ourselves to our targeted places at precisely the same time, just as we did when we arrived here."

"Let's go," Grandpa said.

Chel watched as the two got comfortable and relaxed. She observed them as they transformed themselves from small beings to barely visible images—and then disappeared.

"Don't panic," Chel told herself. "Did he get there? Is he the right size? Is he part butterfly and part human? Is a giant butterfly there?"

She ran directly to the Rainbow Room. Grandpa was there lying on the recliner, waking up, and when she saw him the way he normally appeared, she raced toward him with open arms to give him a huge welcome-back hug.

But Grandpa was startled and immediately repelled. He quickly sat up, twitched oddly, and protected himself with outstretched palms. "Chel, please!" he begged. "Drop the net."

Chel's smile immediately changed to an empty open mouth, and she quickly backed off.

Grandpa ground his teeth, strangely rotated his head, and rolled off his recliner and onto his knees. He quickly glanced in Chel's direction a couple of times and waved his arms like wings; then he got to his feet in a crouched position and moved outside through the screened door. He stood up and looked around in a contorted fashion, still flapping his arms and rotating his head.

He hopped around the yard while continuing to flap his arms rapidly, and he skipped throughout the neighborhood. Chel chased after him for a while. She had increasing difficulty keeping up with him, and she began to notice that he was becoming smaller, and while skipping and flapping, he was able to stay in the air for longer periods. She soon lost him. She began running around the neighborhood, looking from side to side, realizing that her grandfather was becoming a butterfly. Now the middle of the afternoon was upon her.

She stopped and thought. *He can't go too far, can he? I need a plan. He'll be looking for flowers. I need to check out the neighbors' gardens.* She ran back to the house for her butterfly net. *To think I was going to get rid of it!* Then she stopped again and grabbed her cell.

"Exi! You have to meet me at Grandpa's house right now! Get mom to drive you over. It's an emergency. No time to talk now. Just hurry. Oh, and bring your cell phone."

◊

"What's all this about?" Exi asked as Chel met her on the sidewalk near the mailbox.

"Shh," Chel motioned.

Exi whispered as their mom drove away, "You have me worried."

Chel responded, "Let's walk while I explain—and keep a lookout for butterflies. This is going to sound weird but you have to trust me. It's a long story; I'll explain more later. I'm looking for a butterfly, probably still large. Exi . . . Grandpa turned into a butterfly."

Exi stopped. "What! Turned into a butterfly? You got me to stop what I was doing and come all the way over here just so you could play a joke on me?"

Chel clenched her teeth and confronted Exi face to face. "I am *serious*. I said I'd have to explain later because we need the time now to look for Grandpa. You're either with me or not. Which is it?"

Exi backed off. "Okay, okay. Sorry. I'll . . . go along with you." Still unclear, she paused. "Where's Grandma?"

"She left yesterday to visit her brother for a couple of days, thank God."

Exi asked, "What do you want me to do?"

"I see you have your phone. Good. We'll take our street first. You go that way, and I'll go this way. Wherever you see a garden, look for butterflies. Look behind the houses too. If you see a butterfly, call me and I'll be right over with my net."

Five minutes into the search, Chel was combing through the front yard and backyard of her seventh house when her phone rang. "There're two butterflies fluttering around Mrs. Cooper's azaleas. A large blue one and a little pink one."

"Keep your eyes on the large one. Be right there."

Exi was pointing as Chel ran straight up from the sidewalk to the butterfly; her heavy panting did not affect the skill with which she extended the net and whisked in the butterfly."

"Okay," Chel said, gasping for air. "Let's sit down by the sidewalk and see what we have."

She carefully placed her hand around the butterfly, removed it from the net, and examined it closely. With wide eyes and an opened mouth, she turned to face Exi, and then she turned back to the butterfly. With a huge smile, she said, "Hi, Grandpa."

"Let me see," Exi begged. She snuggled up close to the butterfly in Chel's opened palms. "Oh . . . my . . . God . . . It is Grandpa. Tiny. But I see his face. His shirt and shorts. His . . . large wings. Hi, Grandpa. What's going on?"

Chel stood up. "I'll explain on the way back to the house."

◊

Exi placed a small glass end table in front of the chaise in the Rainbow Room, and Chel slowly put Grandpa at the center of the table. The girls sat down, leaning over to face Grandpa closely. Grandpa skittered around a little, not trying to fly. He folded back his wings and stood facing Exi and Chel. He made a sound.

"What?" Both said in unison, leaning over a little farther.

"I'm confused," Grandpa uttered. "What happened?"

"What's the last thing you remember . . . since you became small?" Chel asked.

"Well, I remember . . . behind the house. Yeah, Flutter and I were going to do some astral transplantation to get back to normal. I became completely confused, disordered. Things went sorta . . . blank. The next thing I remember was flying around with a little pink butterfly. I knew I was a butterfly. Had all the characteristics of a butterfly: the need for nectar, the naturalness of flight, and unusual ways of communication that I can't describe. It was shortly after that when you two came for me."

"Grandpa, the transplantation didn't work," Chel said. "You did get transplanted to your recliner, but there was some kind of mix-up, and you started changing to a butterfly. And here you are. I hope this is as far as it goes!"

Grandpa reassured the girls. "I haven't changed any over the past half hour or so."

"Hope you're right," Chel said. "We'll keep an eye on you. Look, on the way here, Exi and I hatched a plan. Exi will tell you about it."

Exi explained. "Grandpa, I'm going up to The Wonderful Place to talk with Uni to see if she can take me to Flutter. Flutter may have some ideas about how to get you back to normal. I'm leaving now and should be back within an hour or so. Chel will be with you 'til I return. Bye, Grandpa." She blew Grandpa a kiss and scampered away.

An hour later, Exi found Grandpa and Chel asleep where she had left them. She tapped Chel's shoulder. "It's dinnertime," she said.

Chel's eyes slowly opened. When she saw Exi, she jerked up from her slumped posture and looked from Grandpa back to Exi. "What did you find out?" She turned to Grandpa. "Grandpa, Exi's back."

"Good news," Exi said. "There may be some hope. Tomorrow at noon, Flutter is coming here, and we'll meet out back, near the wall, where she and Grandpa met. She's bringing another butterfly, some kind of guru, an expert in hypnosis and astral transplantation. He'll talk with Grandpa and try some things to hopefully get him back to normal."

◊

In getting his bearings for the encounter, Grandpa stood, back against the wall, in the exact location where he'd landed in front of Flutter the day before. Exi and Chel were sitting nearby. Out of nowhere, Flutter was in his face. "Hi there," she said, backing off a bit and extending her right arm outward, pointing. "I want you to meet Sagelit." Grandpa looked toward the area where she was pointing and saw nothing for a second—but then he witnessed the spontaneous materialization of a large red-winged butterfly, which so jolted him that his knees buckled.

Flutter continued her introduction. "Sagelit is the master of astral transplantation; he's the one we visit whenever any of us butterflies have a question about it . . . or a problem with it."

"Sorry we startled you . . . It's Roger, isn't it? Hi." Sagelit moved over to shake Grandpa's hand. "That happens sometimes with astral transplantation—a butterfly just appears out of thin air.

"Here's what we're going to do. I'm going to help you repeat the transplantation you tried yesterday, only I'm going to help you fall into a deeper relaxation, a deeper sense of 'non-self'. Know what I mean? You will be conscious and have no awareness of being conscious; you need to be conscious in order to concentrate thoroughly on your target—your recliner, I'm told—while having no sense of anything else, including yourself. But, Roger, more importantly, picture your recliner with you in it. Picture yourself in your recliner. I will be humming to you while you are concentrating; that will facilitate the transformation from you here, in a super-relaxed state with limited consciousness, to you in your recliner. But at some point, you will not be aware of my humming at all. Relax. Do you have any questions?

"How do we start?" Grandpa asked.

"Sit down with your back against the wall or lie down, whichever is more comfortable—so that you won't need to use any muscles for support. You need to be very comfortable. Take some deep breaths, close your eyes, and relax."

Grandpa began relaxing, expelling all physical sensations, focusing only on himself in the recliner, and nothing else. He heard the soft pleasant humming; it sounded as if a chorus of people were humming. It was not easy at first to concentrate on just one thing while such lovely harmony surrounded him, but as he intensified his focusing and relaxation to the utmost, he found that the humming was becoming fainter and the focus on himself in his recliner was becoming more of a vivid image. Finally, he could not hear the humming at all, and the recliner image became a larger three-dimensional object.

"He's gone," Sagelit announced needlessly.

"Let's go see," Exi said.

"Wait," Sagelit said. "A couple of things. First, don't noisily *rush* in; he's still in a relaxed state. Second, if he's still not right, we can try again. Okay?"

Exi and Chel walked through the back door and crossed through the kitchen with Flutter and Sagelit hovering over their shoulders. They heard some activity at the front door, so they stopped. That is the direction that leads through the dining room, past the front door, through the living room, and into to the Rainbow Room. The four peeked around to see.

"Hi, Lyn," Grandpa said, placing Grandma's luggage aside and giving her a big hug. "Hope you had a great visit."

"Hi, honey. Yes, I did. Bill's family is so much fun to visit . . . Wait. What's . . . ? Push your hair back away from your ears. Oh, I get it; working on some new magic, huh? Your ears look like pink butterfly wings. How *realistic!* Wiggle 'em. Oh, that's so great! Roger, fly me away!"

GRANDMA'S DREAM:
ORCHIDS AND PEACOCKS

The doorbell rang unexpectedly in the late morning. "A delivery for Exi and Chel," the deliveryman announced as Exi opened the door.

It was an arrangement of flowers. Full of curiosity, the girls swiftly carried it into the kitchen. As they peeled off the protective wrappings, they first viewed the gorgeous bright white blossoms of tall double stem orchids, and beneath those, they uncovered the clusters of exotic lavender orchids with smiles that revealed their yellow lips framed by rosy hues.

"Wow, they're beautiful," Chel exclaimed. "And for *us?*"

"Yeah, I wonder who sent them," Exi inquired, now looking for a card among the orchids.

What they found instead was startling.

"It's a miniature Grandpa's head stuck onto an orchid stem!" Exi announced. "And he's smiling."

"Yeah, but it's kinda real, like one of those shrunken heads," Chel added. "It's a little scary. Oh my God, it just winked at us!"

Grandpa entered the kitchen. "Hi, girls. I see you've received my gift. No special occasion—I just wanted to express my love for you." He opened his arms and hugged them.

"Thank you, Grandpa," Exi said in appreciation as she and Chel prepared the orchids for the vase. "They're beautiful. But your small head was a bit startling."

"You know I like to surprise. Besides, why not add a little additional beauty to something that's already beautiful?" Grandpa boasted.

The girls never quite fully understood Grandpa's sense of humor.

Grandpa went on to explain how he'd accomplished such a realistic copy of his own head. "When the deliveryman arrived, I pulled him aside, and he helped me do this. I removed the flower from one stem and inserted a round Styrofoam ball onto the stem. Then I used a new product for magicians—called Otrop II."

"How does that work?" the girls asked, intrigued.

He explained. "I covered my face with Otrop II. With my hand, I then wiped it off my face and rubbed it onto the Styrofoam ball. I repeated this a few times to make sure I got as much off my face and onto the ball as possible. Then the ball transformed into the likeness of my face.

"As for the winking eye, well, that's just a reflection trick using small pieces of glass. The eye really does not move at all. But *you* do move, even without realizing it. Seeing the glass eye at slightly different angles as you move creates the illusion of a winking eye."

"Well done, Grandpa," Chel exclaimed.

"You really had us going," Exi added.

"Okay, well, time for lunch. I've been making sandwiches. Grandma will be home soon from the beauty salon."

The girls went to wash up, but when they came back, circumstances had dramatically changed. Grandpa was sitting erect in a kitchen chair. He had orchids flowering out of his neck where his head should have been! They could see at once that this was not one of Grandpa's "funny" jokes. As they were on the verge of outright screaming, they heard a tiny voice.

"Hey! Help! I'm over here!" cried the miniature head in the orchid pot on the counter.

The girls turned toward the arrangement in disbelief. "Oh God—what happened, Grandpa?" Chel screamed.

"I need to be with my body!" demanded Grandpa's head. "Take my head and stem, and stick it in my neck with the other orchids. Please hurry. Grandma has to see me with my head, even if it's smaller."

The girls quickly responded. And then they froze in trepidation—and confusion.

After a pause to think, Chel offered, "I think I know what could have happened, Grandpa. You put too much Otrop on your face and transferred too much of it onto the ball. So the ball eventually turned into your whole face, rather than just receiving an image of your face. And you removed the bloom from one stem and then touched your face to get the Otrop to put on the ball, and so on. You must have transferred some orchid stuff on your face along with some Otrop—or something like that."

Exi burst in. "Why don't you ever read directions, Grandpa? Why do you even mess around with that stuff?"

Grandpa's tiny voice managed a tiny roar. "Easy!"

"Exi is right, Grandpa. Why can't you be smart like Grandma? She would *never* mess around with that kinda stuff!" Chel emphasized.

"Okay, let's all of us calm down a bit and think this through," said the man in the chair, his tiny head enthroned by gorgeous orchids pushing skyward from his neck.

"Hello!" Grandma exuberantly greeted everyone from the kitchen door, home from the beauty salon.

She tap-danced in a quick circle to show off her new look. The girls were once again shocked.

"Grandma, you look like the fanned-out feathers of a giant peacock," Exi delicately announced.

Chel could not resist speaking bluntly. "Your face *is* a peacock!"

Then Grandma noticed Grandpa. "You too?" she sounded off excitedly with glee, bouncing with open arms.

She grabbed Grandpa from the chair, and arm in arm, they skipped off to other regions of the house, leaving the girls aghast.

The girls heard Peacock Head explain to Orchid Head, as they were disappearing through the kitchen doorway, how "the Otrop Corporation now has a new line of beauty products . . ." Exi and Chel stood still for a moment in disbelief.

Then Exi exclaimed, "Those two are really made for each other, aren't they?"

"Yes," Chel responded. "And they deserve each other too."

GRANDPA'S DREAM: THE CURTAIN ROD

Grandpa was having one of his bizarre dreams. Exi, Chel, and some of their friends enthusiastically applauded Grandpa as he completed his magic show in the Rainbow Room. The last trick was the illusion of pushing a solid one-quarter-inch-diameter curtain rod straight though one ear and having it come out of the other, which sparked the small group of admirers.

Grandpa, always believing in safety first, was explaining to the youngsters that it was just a trick and did not involve a real curtain rod. "Look what I'm holding now. Now this is a *real* curtain rod." He held it up as if to enter it into his ear. "Never kid around like this, because accidents can and do happen."

Just then, Grandma, carrying a tray of cookies, kicked open the door leading out into the Rainbow Room, and the force of the door shoved the curtain rod straight though one of Grandpa's ears and halfway out the other. "Ouch! Ouch! Ouch! Ouch!" Grandpa cringed in his weird dream. "That really hurts!"

Grandma dropped the cookies, and everyone began bustling around, trying to figure out what to do about Grandpa, who had a curtain rod protruding out of each ear by more than a foot.

"Are you okay?" Grandma screamed.

"What?" asked Grandpa. "I can barely hear you."

Grandma screamed louder into Grandpa's ear. "We have to get you to the hospital!"

◊

The surgeons said that they couldn't remove the rod. "We have to take you to the hospital's machine shop. Maybe there's something the mechanical engineers can do."

The chief engineer explained the situation to Grandpa. "While the rod cannot be removed, it can be shortened up to your earlobes so that your awkward appearance will be less noticeable. If we drill all the way through the center of the solid rod from one end to the other using our special high-precision equipment, then it will become a hollow tube—and then perhaps you will be able to hear better. This is all speculation, of course, just so you know."

"Do it," snapped Grandpa.

◊

Exi and Chel gave Grandpa big hugs and kisses when he returned home from the machine shop. "We're *so* glad to see you Grandpa. Are you all right now?"

"Yes. I'm fine now. Thank you," Grandpa gloomily answered.

The girls went into a frenzy exploring Grandpa's new fixture. "Look!" Exi exclaimed, scrambling up next to Grandpa's shoulder. "I can see straight through one ear and out the other."

In fact, Grandpa came home hearing better than ever. He soon realized that he could clearly hear things that no one else could hear at all. As he was right-handed, he was also right-eared, meaning that if he directed his right ear toward anything, then he could hear all sounds emanating from that source.

Over the next few days, he realized that the distance of the source of sound didn't matter. From a high hilltop, he could scan his right ear over a neighborhood and hear sounds coming from each passing home.

Grandpa could imagine ways in which the results of his accident could be beneficial, especially in magic shows, in espionage, and in outer space explorations.

"What does it sound like on the moon?" Chel asked.

"Low whispers of wind, the occasional thump of a meteorite."

After some practice, he could listen to sounds on the planet Mars at night. "Low activity, occasional rustles of dust, shifts in ice, and the occasional sounds of something that may best be described as lonely howls and barks," he would explain.

On some nights, Grandpa would scan his right ear through the night skies, avoiding all visible stars and planets, listening for sounds from the deepest reaches of the universe.

Then came the night he heard the voices . . .

"Father, what is the current state of affairs on planet Earth?"

Father answered, "There are good people and evil people, as always. There are productive people and unproductive people. There are smart people and stupid people. But there is still only one true airhead on Earth."

"Oh, you mean the curtain rod guy?" the first voice queried.

"Yes, and tomorrow heaven will open its gates to its first true airhead."

◊

Grandpa instantly awoke, flabbergasted, and quickly staggered for a cold shower.

BOJANGLES

It drizzled on the way to the chapel, but luckily, just before arrival, the sky cleared and the cordial southern sunlight began to brighten the day.

The small chapel sat peacefully in the charming historic district of Columbus, Georgia. The service was simple and graceful, consisting of poetry readings and testimony given by a few of the bereaved, interspersed with flute and organ music, a singing duet, and a prayer. Centered at the front of the altar was the draped box holding the ashes of Grandpa's brother, Keith.

After the service, friends and family gathered at Keith's house for a reception. Grandpa was pleasantly surprised by the number of people who thought so highly of Keith. He and Grandpa had lived several states apart, but they would visit each other once a year. Mostly, Keith would visit Grandpa and his family because he was single and liked to see the grandchildren. But despite the visits and telephone conversations, Grandpa only now learned how deep his roots went in the community. He had the respect of neighbors, faculty, former students, and other friends. He had retired, professor emeritus, from the Art History Department at the university.

In addition to a lifelong collection of paintings and drawings, Grandpa observed a second collection that he knew was particularly precious to Keith. Numerous extraordinary ornamental eggs were placed around the house, and in particular, about a dozen were placed on a table in the second bedroom, which Keith had converted into a study. This served as a reminder of how, as early as his grade school days, Keith created unusual pieces of beauty from hollowed eggs. He painted these and decorated them with ribbons, imitation gems, and other imaginative objects found around the house. As Keith advanced into the world of art, he continued this early interest by collecting Fabrergé and other special ornamental eggs from around the world during his travels.

"Choose one, Dad." Grandpa stood up after being stooped over examining the collection on the table. "What?" Grandpa asked as he turned around. It was Julia, one of Grandpa's daughters. She and his son Randy were the administrators of Keith's estate and beneficiaries of parts of his holdings that included this collection, so they had the final say.

Grandma and Grandpa had a large family—six children, in fact. Julia and Randy lived in different states from them, and neither were parents of Exi and Chel, who lived near Grandma and Grandpa.

Julia explained that each family member could select one of the wonderful pieces to take home.

Grandpa then began a more serious scrutiny of the precious ornaments, and eventually he selected one. He noted that the shape of the ornamental egg and attached stand resembled a manned balloon with a basket hanging below. Its color was a dark purple. The ornament was hollow and constructed in two halves, joined by a hinge, so it opened as a container.

A pearl protruded from the top. Fanning out from beneath the pearl and down onto the ball were fifty or so diamond-like crystals, linked together by an embedded network of thin gold lacing. The small stand was similarly decorated, and the lower part of the stand, a narrow gold-colored column, held up the ornament as if offering it to the sky. Grandpa loved it.

"Thanks, Julia. This is gorgeous. I'll take good care of it."

The next day, Julia drove Grandpa to the airport. They reminisced about Keith and talked about the events of the past few days. Keith had specified that if any immediate family members wanted a small portion of his ashes before they were to be released over the Duke Forest in North Carolina, then they were welcome to have some. Earlier, Grandpa had stated that he would like a small amount.

"Here, Dad," Julia said as she drove. "These are some of Keith's ashes." She handed Grandpa a small tin box, and he received it with sincere gratitude.

"I'll keep them in the ornamental egg and put it on the mantel when I get home." For a moment, they both reflected in silence about that. The conversation about

Keith began to ease off a few miles from the Atlanta airport.

Then Julia asked about Grandma's rings.

About two months earlier, Grandma and one of her fishing friends were fishing in Mile Deep Lake, a well-known spot near home. This was a deep lake. In fact, two years earlier, the local newspaper had reported that the United States Corps of Civil Engineers had measured the deepest part to be equal to the length of a football field, but some still claimed that no one knew its real depth. On that day, Grandma forgot to leave her rings at home. While grappling with the net while pulling in a slippery, fighting bass out of the water with wet hands, she lost her wedding band and diamond engagement ring to the bottom of the lake.

Grandpa explained, "No, there's no way to get them back. I spoke with some water salvage people who told me it's not humanly possible, unless you want to spend a million dollars, and even then, the chance for recovery is close to nil. Moreover, no search permits are permitted until an ongoing environmental study of the lake is completed, which will be at least another year. The rings are buried—history."

Julia sighed in regret. "Gone. That's tough, Dad. You two have really been through it lately. Tell Mom I'm thinking about her. I'll call her soon."

"Yeah, she's climbing out of the doldrums now. It won't carry the memories or the original inscription, but

I promised her something new that she has wanted for a while."

From the car window, Grandpa fixated on the passing labyrinth of spiraled and angled highways near the Atlanta airport, some seemingly vertical, and he enjoyed the last few minutes of the end of Keith's day in private thought with his daughter.

◊

Over the following several days, Grandpa was sluggishly adjusting to his brother's death. He went about his life as usual, tending to his magic shop, being with Grandma, and visiting with his nearby grandchildren. And he did the yard work. But he was not all there. A strange event had happened on the first night after returning home from Keith's memorial service, and it left him haunted.

It was late at night, and he was reading in the living room. He was tired and began to doze off. His head would fall toward his chest; he would catch himself, read more, and doze off again. While in a deep slumber, he was startled over what he heard. It was as if he'd answered a telephone and clearly heard the loud voice: "Hi, Roger. It's Keith. Do you have a second?"

Grandpa instinctively responded, "Yes!" Then silence. No response. Grandpa listened intently for a few seconds and then opened his eyes. "Keith?" He felt hot sweat ooze out onto his forehead. His rate of breathing quickened. "Is this real?" he muttered to himself. He looked around the room. He stood up. He approached the mantel and opened the egg casket. All was in order. Whatever essence of Keith that Grandpa had on the mantel was still there.

Over the next few days, what bothered Grandpa the most was that he did not know what the message meant. His first thought resulted in guilt. Was this a message that Keith felt that Grandpa did not call him enough during his final days of illness? He explored the meaning of the word "second" in Keith's message, feeling that normally Keith would have used the word "minute" instead. Or perhaps it was a warning: *You too have a small amount of time left.*

Over the next few weeks, Grandpa gradually relaxed his grip on this preoccupation. He and Grandma spent enjoyable time with Exi and Chel. Grandma could not explain what he'd heard, but she was of great comfort to him, as he had been to her after she lost her rings. He finally accepted the possibility that that night's voice from Keith was along the lines of a hallucination, although in future moments of reflection, he would have fleeting doubts.

◊

After a month in the doldrums, Grandpa was finding a renewed interest in his work. His business had been sluggish for months, so he had recently hired a part-time consultant magician to help him develop new material for his shows and to help create new tricks to sell in his shop.

"But this guy is good," Grandpa repeated to Grandma, who was questioning the need to spend money to employ a consultant. "Real good. His name is Bojangles."

Bojangles wore colorful, clownish clothes, a fat loud tie, and a striped coat with long tails. He usually wore a top hat, which was useful for various tricks. He sported a thin moustache and a charming smile. And he always carried his banjo strapped on his back, which he often spontaneously played while dancing a quick jig.

One particular Bojangles performance that Grandpa raved to Grandma about was "the spin." He would face an audience and cover his face with the banjo; then he would spin all the way around and face the audience again. But after the spin, Bojangles's face would be replaced by the face of the banjo—and still be donned by the top hat. Then he would raise his arms with his elbows extending outward, as some do when rubbing their eyes, and he would place his fingers on the strings where his nose should be and play a tune. After that, he would spin around the other way and be back to normal.

"Baffling! Purely *baffling!*" Grandpa exclaimed to Grandma. Grandpa related that Bojangles claimed he could even communicate with the dead, and although Grandpa did marvel at Bojangles's outstanding performances, he just could not buy that. Nor could he buy Bojangles's claim that he could turn himself into a stone statue. "You could prove it with a hammer and chisel if desired," Bojangles would amusingly say. Not only didn't Grandpa believe he could do it, but he thought it would be a dumb, boring trick anyway, and he wondered why he would mix this in with his array of wonderful deceptions. Later, when pressed about this, Bojangles said it would be his ultimate performance, and that this is what would happen to him as he died.

Bojangles arrived at Grandpa's magic shop every other day or so and stayed for a few hours. He advised on the development of several new tricks that they both created in the backroom shop and then sold in the store, which was in the front part of the building. Word got around. People from neighboring towns got wind of the clever new tricks being sold at the magic shop. And Grandpa received some new bookings for shows. Business was beginning to pick up.

As time went by, Bojangles occasionally repeated his desire to prove that he could communicate with the dead. He wanted to win the ultimate approval of a respected fellow magician. One clear October afternoon, as the two were loading the van with paraphernalia for a large show in a nearby city, Bojangels firmly declared to Grandpa, "I really can do it! Seriously, you must know a person who has died, someone with whom you wish to communicate. Isn't there some lingering issue with a departed loved one that you wish to resolve?"

"Let's go back into the shop," Grandpa said, finally relenting. "I *am* interested in finding out something from my brother."

They sat down facing each other at the worktable in the shop. Grandpa related his experience with the mysterious brief utterance from Keith that had transpired after arriving home from Keith's memorial service.

"Bojangles, it felt like I had a telephone receiver to my ear, and he just started talking in real time. But we got disconnected. He wanted to tell me something, but when I acknowledged him, well, that was it."

Bojangles listened with interest and asked, "So you want to know what he tried to tell you?"

"Yes, if all this is real. If you really can reach him, you could find out if he tried to communicate something to me. And if so, what?"

Bojangles gave Grandpa the necessary instructions. "Close your eyes and think of Keith. Think of nothing else. Don't be tense. Relax and take a deep breath. Are you relaxing?"

"Yes."

"Okay, I ask that you remain relaxed and put both hands flat down on the table with your fingers stretched out toward me. I am going to do the same, and our fingers will touch. As you concentrate on Keith, some of your feelings of Keith will flow from you, through our fingers, to me. In your mind, ask him your question. Then the genuine strong feelings and question will travel through something in me—some extraordinary part of me—and then leave this world and be received by the one for whom the feelings are expressed: Keith. Then we are connected with him. Anything he expresses will come through my mouth. That's the way it works. Do you understand the general process?"

"Yes."

"Good. Now focus on Keith. Nothing but Keith. I will focus on receiving your thoughts and feelings about Keith—and letting them flow through me."

For a few minutes, the two magicians sat motionless with heads sloped downward, eyes closed, and outstretched fingers on the table—touching.

"Oooooh!" moaned Bojangles suddenly. Grandpa's eyes sprang open. Bojangles's face was white. His eyes were closed, and he was mouthing as if trying to find words.

"Hi, Roger. It's Keith! Do you have a second?" The voice from Bojangles was Keith's. Bojangles's eyes now were widely opened and fixated upward. He was in a trance.

"Yes," Grandpa instinctively bellowed.

After a few seconds of silence, Grandpa was about to say yes again, just to keep connected, when Keith dominated with a firm command.

"Dump my ashes down the drain."

"What?" Grandpa implored in shock.

"I should never have permitted mixed parts of me to be bagged for separate private ownerships, future blind inheritances, and potential sales," Keith said. "It lames me here, in spirit. Tell the others; they will listen." Then the connection was broken.

Grandpa arose, totally stunned.

◊

Bojangles continued to come and go for a couple of months. But due to the sparseness of his part-time work, school schedules and by fate of happenstance, Chel and Exi never met him. But they heard a lot about him and had planned to stop by the magic shop soon to meet the colorful hat-topped swirling jingle man who played his banjo while his black-and-white tap shoes danced on a neighbor's rooftop and, again, down the top of a fifty-yard stretch of fence on the outskirts of town in full view of many wide-eyed townsfolk.

But near the end of Bojangles's time working at the magic shop, Grandpa began to notice that Bojangles was appearing tired. The quality of his work was still excellent, but his production was slower. When Grandpa asked him if he was feeling all right, Bojangles joked, "Fine for a magician who is trying to do the trick that you don't think I can do—turn into stone." He laughed at himself, but Grandpa didn't think it was funny.

During the last day that Grandpa ever spoke with Bojangles, his appearance was slightly different. He had difficulty speaking. Later in the afternoon, he extended his arms toward Grandpa, palms up, and said, "For you." In his two hands, he offered two of the most beautiful ornamental eggs Grandpa ever saw.

Grandpa was taken aback. He looked at Bojangles. He studied his hands, his offerings. Grandpa became tense and confused. Bojangles politely smiled back, but he moved more slowly. Grandpa felt an eerie sensation and continued staring, and Bojangles kept smiling back. Then he reached farther out with his offering. "For you, brother."

Grandpa's mouth dropped open. "Keith!" Grandpa shouted. "Oh God, that's impossible. Am I . . . losing my mind?" After a brief pause, he asked, "My God, Keith, is that really you?"

Keith responded, "The message I was trying to give you that night was cut off. You heard 'Do you have a second?' What I meant to relate to you, in addition to the part about my ashes, was a catchy little conversational beginning: 'Do you have a second chance at life on Earth?' Then I was going to follow up with 'I did.'

"But I'm glad we were cut off. After thinking more carefully about it, I decided I would prefer to pay you a visit. I am not all Keith. Well, I am mostly. I have Keith's memories. But I have a different personality, different characteristics, and idiosyncrasies. I can't explain it completely, but I know from where I was that occasionally some humans who are dead on Earth do get placed back as humans in some slightly altered state. I did not want you thinking of me as Keith and calling me Keith. I wanted to 'out magic' you, for your benefit, unannounced as a master of real magic, and that's just not Keith. You wouldn't have permitted it.

"Oh, and thanks for solving the ashes problem. And one other thing—the consulting money you paid . . . me is in your . . . ornamental . . . egg . . . on . . . the mantel."

At that instant, Bojangles stood permanently motionless—solid stone.

Later, Exi and Chel came by the shop to meet Bojangles for the first time and to poke about as usual. Grandpa was quiet and reflective, but attentive. Bojangles stood stationary in the center of the shop.

Chel exclaimed, "Wow, Grandpa, this is a neat new statue! Looks real. Kinda reminds me of Great-Uncle Keith."

The girls were in awe of this creation, facing them and smiling at them.

"Yeah," Exi agreed, instinctively smiling back at Bojangles. She circled him carefully, examining his unusual attire and admiring the detailed carvings on the banjo strapped to his back.

She looked at the ornamental eggs poised in his hands. Pointing to each, one at a time, she innocently quipped, "One life—and another life. What an offering."

The magician, looking directly into Keith's eyes while giving a nodding approval, reflected.

"Right. The holder of two different lives on Earth . . . Oh my God! What a trick!"

◊

That night, Grandpa had quite a story to tell Grandma, but she wasn't buying it. "I know he's gone," she said. "But the stone statue bit—forget about it. It's no more unusual than a lot of stuff you have there."

She offered her insight that with all the talk, he never did perform one trick having to do with the paranormal. "Getting down to it, he never did perform a stunt that any other talented magician couldn't do," she said.

"Even the voice you heard that night could have been a hallucination, and he just capitalized on it. He simply cannot do what is humanly impossible. He was what you hired him for: *a paid consultant.*"

At that, Grandpa remembered what Bojangles had said about the money being in the urn. Earlier, he had wondered how the bills could be compressed in order to fit inside such a small space.

"Bojangles put the money I paid him in the urn." Grandpa got up to retrieve the money. "Maybe this will help convince you. We both know he's never been in the house, with you here most of the time and the alarm system and all. I'll prove the 'human impossibility' to you." But Grandma was not convinced.

"Oh—a magician could sneak in, I bet. But go see if it's there anyway."

He went into the living room and noted that the money was actually in an envelope under the urn. But naturally, he peered into the urn.

What he saw made this the most profound and, simultaneously, the happiest moment in Grandpa's life. He returned slowly to the Rainbow Room, where they had been sitting, and extended both hands to her, opened, as if making an offering. One hand presented Grandma's diamond ring, and the other offered her wedding ring.

Grandma finally came around . . . "Oh my God! What a trick!"

MIRROR, MIRROR ON THE WALL

The angry storm had passed, and the midafternoon sun began to pacify the fall day. Shoppers were now reappearing on the sidewalks and parking lot. Exi and Grandma were carrying their shopping bags to the car when Exi began feeling that Grandma was preoccupied with something.

"Exi, when we get in the car, I'm going to tell you about a very unusual experience I just had in the dressing room."

They had been shopping at Miracles, Grandma's favorite clothing store, so that Exi could choose a present for herself—a reward for an especially good grade on a major math test. As a result, Exi had made two choices from the large collection of sweaters, and Grandma bought some slacks and a lightweight jacket, on sale, for herself.

Grandma sighed and changed the subject. "Maybe these will make me look pretty again."

"What are you talking about, Grandma? You're always pretty."

In recent months, Grandma had spent some moments in the doldrums. The pounds and the wrinkles that she perceived were not welcomed, but she did appreciate her life. "Thank you Exi. I'm too hard on myself, aren't I?" Grandma smiled.

It was the typical fun outing that Exi and Grandma enjoyed together, until near the end of it. Exi first noticed the change in Grandma's appearance at the checkout counter, but she simply couldn't put her finger on it. After they placed their items in the trunk of the car and Grandma closed the lid, Exi asked, "Grandma, do you feel all right? I mean, somehow you look a little different."

"Sure, I feel fine, other than the frightening experience that I'm trying to find the words to tell you about. What looks different about me?"

"I don't know." Exi starred at Grandma. "Did you comb your hair differently while you were in the dressing room or something?"

"No. Why?"

"Because it looks switched or something. Like the hair that comes out more on this side now comes out more on that side," Exi said, pointing.

Grandma faltered. "Don't be ridic . . . !" Her voice trailed off as she put her hands on her head. "What now?" She patted both sides of her head in confusion. "No. It's right." But some part of her knew that Exi was correct also.

Scanning seriously now, Exi gave her the once-over.

"Grandma . . . wait. The rings you wear on you left hand are now on your right hand!"

Grandma stretched out her hands and gazed at them. She looked at Exi and was reflective in her response. "You know, a few minutes ago in Miracles, when I was signing the credit card slip, I had the strangest sensation about my hands. I was kind of *pushing* the pen along awkwardly, instead of *pulling* it as I'm used to. And my handwriting seemed different."

"Grandma, you were signing with your left hand and you are right-handed! Show me which hand you signed with."

Grandma raised her left hand.

Exi countered, "Which hand do you usually sign with?"

Grandma again raised her left hand.

"But, Grandma, you're right-handed!"

Grandma was still confused. "Isn't this my right hand?"

"No, Grandma, it's your left!"

◊

That afternoon, Grandpa met the two at the parking lot to intervene. Grandma could not find the coordination to back out of the parking space. He was terribly worried that Grandma had experienced a stroke or some kind of psychological trauma. When they arrived home, Grandma walked slowly up the walkway to the front door, alternatively examining the left and right side of the house as if puzzled by a twisted environment. Yet she could talk and think perfectly fine.

Resting in the living room, the three had a chance to discuss the matter. Grandma wanted to explain her experience in the dressing room, and Grandpa was strongly urging that she get medical help.

"Wait! Listen," Exi asserted. "I know what happened to you, Grandma!"

Grandma and Grandpa, with piqued interest, awaited Exi's diagnosis.

"You have right-left reversal."

"What?" exclaimed Grandpa. "What's right-left reversal?"

"The parts of the body that were on your left side went to your right side, and vice versa," Exi explained. "You know how your image is in the mirror, right? Well, if that image becomes a person, that person would be exactly you, except that person's right and left sides would be reversed."

Grandma was becoming increasingly curious. "Do you mean I became my mirror image?"

"Yeah, or something like that."

"I don't understand," Grandma replied. "That's not possible."

Exi explained. "Many things in this world that seem impossible on the surface may indeed be possible. These may have simple explanations, once they are understood, or they may be profoundly difficult. I went to the science fair last month, and one of the most interesting parts was a demonstration of the magnetic polar reversal. Every few million years, the north and south poles reverse. Instead of pointing north, the dial of a compass will reverse and point south. Grandma, maybe you're like Earth's poles in some mysterious personal universe."

Grandma's demeanor did indicate an understanding. She simply remained reclined in her chair, facing Exi.

Grandpa raised the important question for Grandma. "What were the last things you did before having the feeling something wasn't right?"

"Well, that's what I want to explain. I was going to tell Exi about this horrible experience I had in the store, but that was when all this questioning about being right-handed or left-handed and such took place in the parking lot. It was like a nightmare, but worse. Before my experience at the checkout counter, I was in the dressing room trying on the jacket. There was this loud booming thunder, and there must have been a huge bolt of lightening—an enormous brightness flashed through."

"Oh, yeah, I know!" Exi broke in. "Nothing before then?"

"No."

Exi came to a conclusion, followed by a question. "Your right-left reversal happened in the dressing room. What else was there other than a mirror?"

"Not much: lights, a bench, hooks to hang clothes on. The lights flickered, and the walls of the little dressing room rattled like crazy. The mirror, though, reacted in an especially sinister way. It flickered from black and gray to blinding bright. All this happened instantly. I was terrified. I had been looking at myself in the mirror. I felt dizzy. During a brief gray period, instead of my mirror image, I saw the wide face of a scowling fanged demon with enormous round red eyes—like in a horrible nightmare. And its face was divided. One side was a bright red, and the other was silver."

Grandma paused and took a deep breath to regain her composure. "It thrust its head out of the mirror right in front of me and stuck its right hand through its right ear, all the way through its head and out the left ear, and then it crazily shook its head. It stuck its left hand through its left ear, all the way through its head and out through the right ear, and shook again. Then each hand grabbed the opposite ear and pulled those ears back all the way through to the opposite side of the head and . . . *pop!* The demon yanked both sides of its head to opposite sides. It looked like a bloodied brain. Its hands went to the bloody mess and pinched it and twisted it in odd ways and, behold, the face was there again, but the red and silver sides were reversed. Then it grinned at me—and I mean a huge grin—and howled, continuing to stare at me and shake its hands and arms all over the place. Still glaring and grinning at me, it backed up and . . . and just disappeared back through the mirror. Then the thunder and lightning ceased and all was normal again—except for me."

Grandpa and Exi were sitting before her, listening in a state of near disbelief.

But Grandpa was also concerned about her in another way. Recently, on a few occasions, she had mentioned what she referred to as her "aging appearance." She never dwelled on it, but during the few times she mentioned it, she was a little lost in thought. Grandpa buried his forehead into his left hand and quietly whispered, "And now this on top of that!"

Before reaching out for medical help, they agreed that a visit to the dressing room was in order. Grandpa hypothesized that lightning struck the building in an area near the dressing room, and a strong electric charge crossed the surface of the mirror while she was looking into it. Perhaps this had something to do with her exceptional transformation, as if Grandma disappeared while her mirror image stepped out of the mirror and took over.

That evening, Grandpa and Exi prepared for a morning visit to Miracles. Mainly Grandpa tested his arc and poles that he used for certain performances, for a trick that required a highly charged conduction of electricity from one pole to the other. With this, the plan was to repeat the effect of lightning crossing the same mirror under the same conditions at the same time, with Grandma looking into the mirror in the same way, with the wild hope that another right-left reversal would happen and make her normal.

◊

They picked up Chel the next morning and explained the predicament to her. As they began turning into Miracles' parking lot, Chel was the first to notice. "God, what happened?" They pulled up closer and got out of the car.

All fixated on two patrol cars with flashing lights, people meandering around, a large roped off area, and one huge tractor trailer delivery truck mashed into the front right side wall of Miracles, directly outside the dressing room. No one was injured, and nothing was damaged on the inside—except for the mirror, which was shattered into a million pieces.

Upon recognition of this fate, Grandma plopped herself down on the damp parking lot asphalt. "The dogs of space and Earth arise to opportunity, and those with brains not warped by eventual failed theory but wrapped by real geometry in six point seven dimensions will succeed as rat replacements in tangible nonexistence spelled 'null,' but for two *l*'s, a *u*, an *n*, and an *a*, and except for the bathwater of the petroleum, I bathed and bathed the poor pet out for years or years, and I expelled the water and the gas and drank the beach in the backyard until I became me."

An ambulance arrived in short order and rushed her away.

◊

After a few hours at the local hospital, Grandma had recouped enough to speak somewhat coherently, and then she was transferred to the state university hospital, which maintained better-equipped facilities for diagnosing unusual or complex cases. No one had an explanation for her right-left reversal, but the doctors more urgently focused on her temporary gibberish, which, while still rare, was a more familiar presentation. Grandpa knew the docs would misclassify this as a psychiatric case—maybe stress related—failing to realize that paranormal forces might be at work. But he figured that maybe there was a medical person somewhere in this world who knew something about this. *What else can I do?* Grandpa wondered.

The doctors were reassuring. They held a conference and made some calls. Ultimately, they located a doctor in another state who was both a psychiatrist and a neuroscientist. He was well known in the medical community not only for his research in severe confusion disorders and other mental abnormalities but also for his research in a region of the brain that separates the right and left hemispheres. This region is the "corpus callosum." He had conducted extensive research and made many important discoveries regarding properties and purposes of parts of the corpus callosum. Upon learning of Grandma's unique pathological dilemma, he became extremely intrigued and rearranged his complex schedule in order to fly to the university hospital to meet her. He promised state-of-the-art medical examinations and treatment upon his arrival.

Grandpa, Exi, and Chel were in the hospital room visiting Grandma when two local doctors accompanied the famous doctor to Grandma's room. "Hello Lyn, I'm Dr. Steadman," the renowned visiting doctor announced.

Dr. Steadman learned the details of what happened and gave Grandma a brief initial examination. The others in the room could not help but notice how this man, who probably had the most expertise of anyone else in this neurological specialty, was genuinely motivated to understand what happened to Grandma and to bring her back to normal.

The next two days were filled with neurological tests, vision tests, psychological tests, brain scans, and other kinds of examinations. By the end of the second day of testing, Dr. Steadman was prepared to offer a course of action.

"I want to tell you about the only other experience I have had regarding a case that was similar to yours," Dr. Steadman told Grandma. "About five years ago, a man was brought to my attention. This man, Stuart, suffered the extraordinary experience of the right-left reversal."

The family and the other doctors in the room were now eager to hear about what was promising to be to a most intriguing and strange experience—and course of action.

"Stuart told me he was visiting a friend who lived in Vancouver, Canada. This friend's name was Mr. Otto. People simply refer to him as Otto. Otto had recently moved to the west coast of Canada from Japan. He lived with his wife in a large modern house that they had designed and built in a quiet residential area of Vancouver that was populated largely by Japanese people. The homes were gorgeous, reflecting the customs of Japanese landscaping and architecture."

Dr. Steadman explained that he had visited Otto, and he described the home's physical environment.

"The interior of Otto's home was spacey and bright. On the right side of the house as you faced it was what Otto called the 'mirror room.' The room featured a large mirror, on the left as you entered. A sliding curtain hung from a track a few feet in front of the mirror. Attached to each side of the mirror was a large metal plate, forming a pair of electric poles. An enormous electric charge could be made to bolt like lighting from one pole to the other, crossing over the surface of the mirror. At the back of the room, on the right as you entered, stood a panel of controls. One control was used to turn the apparatus on and to send a charge and a dial was used to adjust the strength of the charge. This is the process for causing right-left reversal."

"And let me guess," Grandpa interjected. "Stuart did it!"

"Yes, accidentally," Dr. Steadman replied. "Let me give you a brief history. Otto somehow discovered the mirror in Japan and brought it with him to Canada. He found it in an old antique shop. Also, he barely noticed that hidden on the back of the mirror was an old document describing some special use for the mirror. He liked the mirror because of some of its attractive features and properties. For one, inscribed on top of its wooden frame was the infinity sign—look here; it's drawn like this . . ." He drew this symbol: ∞. "If you draw it without interruption, you will complete it where you began it—an interesting symbol for infinity. Otto is a symbolist—quite an interesting occupation.

"Anyway, Otto and Stuart would experiment with reversing objects such as drill bits, small motors, radios, portable computers, and other devices to see how they would work after reversal. They even used rats. If you reverse an object and then zap it a second time, you transform it back to normal again. Their interest was in the potential commercial applications of right-left conversions. Having the only known method of doing this, as far as they knew, they figured that if they could find an application, they would soon be millionaires—or billionaires."

"What happened to Stuart?" Chel reminded Dr. Steadman.

"Oh, yes. One day they made a tragic mistake. They planned to reverse a mannequin just to take photos to make detailed comparisons on how different the original and reversed mannequins would be. They placed the mannequin in front of the mirror and closed the curtain. The curtain was made of a thick, tightly woven material for the protection of anything or anyone not to be reversed. The curtain itself was reversed for each application of the high voltage apparatus, but that didn't matter. What mattered was that Stuart felt compelled to record the mannequin's reversal, so he slipped a flexible recording tube under a far corner of the curtain to film the events. That was fine. He was safe because he did not expose himself directly to the mirror to view the right-left reversal as it was happening."

Dr. Steadman took a breath in wonder. "Then, an hour later, when Stuart viewed the film that he had recorded, he suddenly right-left reversed. Simple as that. By the way, he too later experienced a temporary psychotic outburst of nonsense—a paroxysm, as we call it." The doctor scribbled a reminder on his notepad to the effect that paroxysm appeared to be a sign of this rare complex.

"My God," Exi exclaimed. "But Otto and Stuart could reverse the reversal, like you've explained, so what was the problem?"

"There is a special difficulty with humans," the doctor pronounced. "The document that accompanied the mirror explained that nonhuman objects could be reversed a second time to return to normal. But humans have high-order brains that can reason. Anything with a brain capable of reasoning must have the capacity for understanding right-left reversal and must be thinking about it, and explaining it to himself or herself at the time that the electric charge is passing through, in order for it to work. The person must be focused precisely on answering what the document refers to as the 'key question.' I'll explain the key question like this—"

"That doesn't make any sense," Chel interrupted. "Why should humans be singled out for extra requirements just to make the second reversal work?"

"That's a good question, Chel," Dr. Steadman said. "As far my colleagues and I can determine, each human has two sophisticated hemispheres, one on each side of the interior of the skull, that make up the brain, and these hemispheres relate to one another through the corpus callosum. The two hemispheres communicate, as it were. That's what makes us tick. Evidently, this 'communication' is somehow related to the reason for the extra step, in humans, in order to be properly reversed back to normal. Other animals and inanimate objects don't need this."

Grandpa needed clarification. "What's this extra step . . . this understanding of right-left reversal . . . this so-called 'key question' that must be answered for all this to work?"

"Picture yourself standing in front a mirror." Dr. Steadman needed to have everyone understand the key question, whose correct answer must be contemplated in front of Otto's mirror at the precise time that the charge leaps across, before a second successful reversal could be completed.

"Suppose that your mirror image becomes a real person. Imagine your image stepping out of the mirror, turning around and standing next to you. That person will be exactly like you physically, in every way except one. That exception is this: Where your right arm is on you, the new you—your mirror image—will have your left arm. Where your left arm is on you, the new you will have your right arm. This applies to every part of your body. Where your right side is, your mirror image will have your left side. There is a complete right-left reversal. This is what happened to Lyn, except her real self, not just her image, was reversed. The key to becoming successfully reversed the second time, in order to return back to normal, is to stand in front of the mirror and, at the time the charge is leaping across the mirror, contemplate deeply the *answer* to the key question: *Why does your mirror image get right-left reversed, but your mirror image does not get top-bottom reversed?*"

The four listeners pondered this for a moment. Exi was the first to speak out. "Yeah, that's right. Right and left are reversed, but up and down aren't. Why's that?"

"Exactly! That is the key question." Dr. Steadman continued. "You must be engaged in explaining to yourself the answer to that key question. That is, according to the document, you must be thinking about the answer so that the process of reversal can happen. But people don't seem to know the answer. Stuart stood before the mirror as high voltage shot around it and deeply thought about what he thought was the right answer. Evidently he had a wrong answer, because he remains reversed."

The doctor looked down and paused. "I wish I had the answer. I have asked mathematicians, scientists, philosophers, and others, but they say they don't know or that they will think about it and get back to me, or whatever. No one knows. One philosopher said that there are some actual unanswerable questions—not just *unanswered* but *unanswerable* questions—about our nature and even suggested that this 'key question' may be one of them. Even Otto has given this a lot of thought from the symbology viewpoint."

"What about that demon that tormented me?" Grandma pleaded. "If the mirror is full of those things, I'd rather go un-reversed."

Dr. Steadman explained. "According to the document and to Stuart's different experience, whatever you are experiencing at the time of reversal, some magnification of it possesses you for a moment. Stuart experienced hundreds of mannequins wildly chasing him. Looking into the mirror, perhaps you were focused—well, we have talked about some of your concerns—on your appearance, and then, shocked by the thunder and lightning at that instant, your thoughts immediately manifested themselves as this demon."

He momentarily reflected on what he had said. "That's what I think, anyway. The answer to the key question is the important thing right now. Call me if you find it, and I'll make the arrangements with Otto."

The four were left staring at each other as Dr. Steadman left the room.

"Let's find the answer," Exi demanded.

◊

Exi was obsessed by the key question. That night, she deeply wondered about what makes "right-left" so fundamentally different from "up-down." *Is up-down different from top-bottom? What happens if I lie down in front of a mirror? Is right-left reversed then? What about up-down or top-bottom when I'm lying down? What is right-left reversal reversing around? What would top-bottom reversal look like? Is there a front-back reversal? Does gravity play a role? Does symmetry play a role? How do I understand this?* The hour was late. She was probing for answers to these questions as she drifted off . . .

Twinkle, twinkle, little star. The winking face in the shining moon was face-to-face with her—and whispering. The smiling moon introduced her to the starlit sky as it reached out to embrace her. This was the introduction to a profound dream. Exi drifted into a space of thin bright air where hundreds of randomly placed people were rotating slowly and were otherwise motionless. Some were rotating around their vertical axes like dancers on ice, twirling in slow motion with arms and faces reaching upward. Others were rotating around their right-left horizontal axes, like gymnasts rolling forward alternatively landing on their hands and feet in slow motion. There were colorful clowns doing sideways cartwheels like rolling stars, revealing yet another axis of orientation. This was a vastly mystifying and fascinating performance. But in the deeper imagination of her dream, Exi sensed that a profound meaning was attached to all of this. *How I wonder what you are.*

◊

Heads turned to watch the foot race down the hospital corridor first thing in the morning.

"Grandma, Grandma!" Exi announced as she and Chel screeched into Grandma's room. "We're going to Vancouver."

"You have the answer, do you?" Grandma asked with reservation. "After Dr. Steadman's enlightenment, I began to wonder if there even was an answer."

Exi persisted. "I'm going to explain it to you, Grandma. It's really simple once you understand it." Exi shrugged her shoulders and approached. "It has to do with how we move on this planet, and how the point of reference for left and right is fundamentally different from the point of reference for up and down. I'll explain." Chel turned and took two steps back and closed the door.

◊

In a few hours, the four were on a plane with Dr. Steadman, destined for Vancouver.

Grandma found Otto's home neat and bright, just as Dr. Steadman had described it. Otto was pleasant and prepared for the visit. He was eager to see if the reversal would work. "The mirror room is right this way," he politely offered as he led the way.

Otto closed the curtain, separating Grandma from the others. Otto reminded the others not to peek or do anything to be exposed to the mirror when he produced the electric charge. He gave Grandma a minute to start concentrating on the reason why her reflection in the mirror was right-left reversed but not top-bottom reversed. She was in deep concentration when the flashes cracked across the surface of the mirror with lightening-like forces. After a long ten seconds, it was over. All was quiet and still for a few moments.

"Wow!" Grandma exclaimed. "This is beautiful. Don't open the curtain yet."

She was silent for a minute. It was as if she weren't there. But finally she announced, "I simply cannot leave yet. I have to explore this. You all fly back home. I'll be there when you get there."

But the strangest statement was yet to come.

"When you get home, just wait for me in the bedroom, in front of my dressing room mirror."

Then silence.

When Otto opened the curtain, she was not there.

◊

The beautiful hidden world "behind" all viewing sides of mirrors is not found by looking *behind* a mirror. One must go *through* a mirror, so to speak; this new world is submerged deeply beyond the thin viewing surface of all mirrors. In some profound way, the *non-viewing* sides of all mirrors on Earth are connected and form a remarkable space that is not observable from our world, which contains only the *viewing* sides of mirrors.

Grandma was relaxed, smiling, and floating in the wondrous space. She soon found that this world gave of itself. Beings from Earth or elsewhere (other civilized worlds in the galaxies contain mirrors too) would absorb knowledge and other aspects of this beautiful place. She inexplicitly knew that huge streams of thin air flow through the denser air, forming an enormous network of interconnecting invisible passageways. The denser air forms invisible walls, floors, and ceilings for these passageways, whose interiors contain the lighter air. Through the passageways, the trillions of places of mystery and beauty are accessible.

Grandma floated though the light air corridors by simply thinking about a direction in which she wanted to travel. She witnessed magnificent sparkling spheres of magical geometrical shapes sprinkled throughout the space. Stars and moons, large and small, were far and near. She saw that the space was crisscrossed with several spectacular objects best described as enormous rainbows, but they moved and they faded, in and out. She found that silence was broken only by faint distant sounds of heavenly music, the likes of which had never been experienced on Earth. And for all these objects, she absorbed profound knowledge about them.

Orientation to direction and time is altered for the few who have ever been to this hidden world. There is the vague but pleasant acquaintance of the fifth dimension. The fifth dimension provides for a special beauty. It creates that extra part of the completeness that we on Earth cannot imagine because we are limited to experiencing only four dimensions. And a person passing through this world inside all mirrors will absorb an element of fifth-dimensional beauty, if that person's soul possesses an inner beauty. The fifth dimension is absorbed and extends outward, to the body's surface, whatever inner beauty is there.

Grandma saw the brightly silver sparkles spread throughout this space of many horizons. She instinctively knew that they were the reverse sides of mirrors and were not visible from Earth. Some of them that sparkle from afar actually represent clusters of millions of mirrors, and up close one can reason that they are the reverse sides of mirrors in a dense city, forming millions of starlike shining points. Vast vacuities indicate forests and seas on Earth (or elsewhere), wherein mirrors are not present. Grandma observed some sparkling points flying; these are the reverse sides of mirrors in cars, airplanes, and other vehicles on Earth.

Occasionally during her two-day journey through the world behind all mirrors, Grandma observed groupings of extraordinary narrow light beams aimed in many directions, interspersed with showers of bright sparks. She knew this to be the reverse side of a broken mirror. She was fortunate to witness the rare sight of an actively breaking mirror; the fifth dimension reflects this activity as canopies of huge rainbows bursting out, covering all of space with incredible colors, shimmering densely and crazily, for the few seconds that it lasts.

During her first day of floating in elation, Grandma sensed a presence for a while, and then she realized she had a floating visitor. She looked vaguely like a hazy light yellow smiley face. "Hi, I'm your guardian; my name is Misty. I'm here to keep you company and to converse with you about this special place we're in. Lyn, first I must tell you that soon you will feel great beauty surrounding you." Misty spun around at a high-spin velocity and transplanted herself on the other side of Grandma.

Grandma was happy floating around with Misty. With her abnormal absorption of knowledge and Misty's help, she knew where she was with reference to any mirror on Earth. She had been given a mind's eye for all shapes and locations of all passageways and their many intersections in this magnificent realm behind all mirrors. And she and Misty could float faster than the speed of light if they wished. Grandma was experiencing boundless freedom in a beautiful new place. She no longer felt any concern over her reversal or her appearance.

Soaring throughout, up and under, right and left, fast and slow, laughing and singing, blending with the music and color, they were experiencing bliss in the boundless beauty.

Grandma was experiencing—she was doing—the fifth dimension.

Near the end of their voyage, Misty said, "We'll fly around here again in the future to celebrate our good time here. Then I will explain more. You are one of the few beings who have ever been selected—yes, selected—to visit this place. Selected because of your beautiful soul, your inner beauty. You have absorbed much knowledge about the world behind all mirrors—but there is more.

"When you want to visit, just look deeply into any mirror, looking beyond your image, and whisper 'Misty' a few times. And no, you don't need to be thinking of the answer to the key question; you're beyond that now."

◊

Grandpa, Exi, and Chel arrived home from Vancouver and dashed directly to Grandma's dressing room mirror. They turned on the light and waited tensely with vague expectations. But they didn't wait long before they saw a leg lifting toward them, out of the mirror. Then came an arm, and then the front side of Grandma emerged.

All of Grandma stepped right up to the three pairs of ballooned eyes. "Hi," she announced with a beautiful smile. "I am home and I am reversed."

It had worked. She was right-left reversed for the second time, which put her physical symmetry back to normal.

But the three could not take their eyes off her. Grandma was now extraordinarily beautiful. She always had been beautiful, and she appeared to be back to normal now, but there was something remarkably different about her. None of the three silent observers were able to pinpoint specific differences, but she was more beautiful than anyone they had ever seen. But how? At the same time, she looked just like Grandma. But the more they stared, the more the beauty captivated them. *Absolute* beauty. A tear of wonderment came to each eye.

"Well?" she asked, spreading arms slightly forward, palms out, as if introducing all of herself.

The three were speechless.

She softly lowered her hands and curtsied, giving a slight swirl and a radiant smile. She had only one thing to say.

And she winked when she asked, "Who's the fairest of them all?"

THE SECRET
ABOUT THE MAGIC SHOP

Grandpa was quietly working in the back room of his magic shop on a bright June afternoon when he heard an extremely loud boom. It sounded like a tossed cinder block smacking the wood floor. He spontaneously raised his head to face the door to the front store area—the boom still lingering.

Such interruptions of the workshop's serenity were not new to Grandpa. He had heard mysterious sounds in his shop on three or four occasions over the past couple of months, and about a year ago, he heard a sharp bang followed by what sounded like tinkling glass, making him think that someone had slammed a hammer into a glass countertop. The sounds occurred in varied places within the magic shop. This time, he was in the workshop and sensed that the sound came from the front store area, but when he checked it out, he saw nothing. If a customer had entered or left, the bell hanging on the door would have alerted him. He glanced around again, shrugged his shoulders, and returned to the workshop.

An hour later, he heard what sounded like something scratching on a rough plastic surface, but this time the sounds came from above. Grandpa and Grandma had converted the attic into a furnished apartment, but they had not yet rented it out. Grandpa went outside to the stairway and climbed up to the apartment; again, all seemed in order. But twice in one day was too much for Grandpa. He closed up early and went to Radio Shack, where he inquired about a listening device—a bug. He learned that he could purchase one from a spy shop, and there happened to be one fifteen miles to the west. Finally, he returned to his shop and set up the monitoring device near the back wall of the front store area, secluding it under the cash register, which was centrally located within the magic shop.

He went home with the listening device so that he could monitor and record any sounds in the shop. Also, he wanted to discuss this with Grandma and, with her, devise a plan for discovering the source of these uncanny sounds.

Grandma had known about the sounds, but now Grandpa gave her more detail. "Something could be living in the walls," Grandma suggested. "Maybe we should call an exterminator."

Grandpa responded, "You're probably right . . . but I don't know; it just seems really odd to me. The sounds are so varied and loud that I just can't imagine something that large living in the walls. But, remember, over a year ago we found that the walls of the shop are twice as thick as normal walls, and we could find no reason for that. And today, as I was climbing the stairs, I sensed that the space between the store ceiling and the apartment floor was also wider than usual." Grandpa paused in thought. "Maybe something large does live in the walls. An exterminator may be helpful. Yes, we should call Jay. He's done good work here at the house, despite his personality quirks."

Grandma pointed to the listening device. "Let's turn it on and record whatever comes through."

Grandpa flicked the ON button, and they both immediately heard some rustling sounds. They also heard what sounded like whispers and an occasional *knock* or *thump*. They stared at each other in bewilderment. Then came the bombshell. A clear sentence in a high-pitched voice burst out: "Hey, Clarence, found a large grub in the parking lot!"

Grandpa jumped to his feet and felt his pocket for his car keys.

"Wait," Grandma said. "It may be dangerous. Let's call nine-one-one."

"I may do that, but I have to get to the shop!" On the way out, he turned back to Grandma and said, "Keep listening to the device."

Grandma kept listening to the same cluttered sounds and an occasional English word. Three minutes after Grandpa left the house, she heard a commotion of high-pitched overlapping voices. "He's here! He's come back! Quick! Back in the walls! Quick! Quiet! Quiet . . ."

There was silence for a few seconds, until the hanging bell dinged as the door opened, after which Grandpa's voice came through. "Can you hear me, Lyn? Don't answer. I can't hear you. I've turned on the lights. All seems fine here. I'll check the workshop . . . Okay, it's fine back here too. Nothing out of place. Even smells normal. Hmm. I'm puzzled . . . and worried. Okay, I'll be home in a few minutes. Oh! Here's a large grub worm near the counter. It looks dead. I'll leave it here till tomorrow, just as an experiment. See ya in a bit."

Back home, having listened to the recording, he murmured, "Maybe this *is* a police matter." He pondered for a moment and said, "But let's try Jay first, just to get a better idea of what's going on. I'll call him first thing in the morning."

◊

Grandpa arrived at the shop at eight thirty and noted that the grub worm was gone. Responding to Grandpa's urgent request, Jay arrived at the shop at nine. "I don't know quite how to put it, Jay, but I hear noises. I suspect something's living in the walls." Grandpa did not want to admit to also hearing English-speaking voices, but after some reflection, he decided to be up front and tell the whole story.

Without saying a word, but with raised eyebrows and a subtle smirk, Jay put an ear to the wall that separated the workshop and store areas. "I hear nothing." He removed a stethoscope from his bag, put the earpieces in his ears, and placed the receiver on the wall. "Shh . . . I *do* hear a faint sound. Don't know what it is, though."

Stepping back and removing the stethoscope, he said, "We're going to have to cut a hole in the wall and peek in. I can repair it later, and it'll look like before. Let's do it from the workshop side in case a customer comes in."

Jay drilled a small hole in the wall, and then he inserted the narrow blade of his electric saw to widen the hole so that he could insert his flashlight. When he turned on the saw, the electric power in the store died, and the saw quit working. They heard the high, shrill voice from within the wall: "Get that horrid thing out of here!"

Jay immediately withdrew the saw and backed off. Grandpa backed off also, fearfully asking, "Who said that?"

All was quiet for a few seconds and then the high-pitched voice from within the wall exclaimed, "If you keep that saw blade away, we'll turn the electricity back on. You don't have to destroy a wall when there are hidden doors to most of the walls around here. You think these walls exist only for the magic shop? Well, they're walls for our home too."

Jay, an impulsive character, reacted strongly. "I gotta see what's in there." He ran to his truck, grabbed his crowbar, ran back in, and whacked a gaping hole in the wall. He raised his flashlight to ram it in, but just then, a small but strong humanlike hand and forearm poked out of the hole and snatched the flashlight from Jay. Then the arm extended farther out and threatened to smack Jay in the head with the flashlight; instead, the arm flung it across the room, and it hit the corner of a sturdy worktable, shattering the lens and the bulb.

"I'm outta here!" Jay cried out, clearly shaken. "And don't worry, I ain't telling nobody 'bout this. I don' want no trouble—no way!" He quickly gathered his belongings and on wobbly legs waddled out to his truck and left. Then the power was restored.

"You should make sure he doesn't speak of this, or your shop will become the center of some kind of investigation," the voice from within the wall said. There was a notable pause before the inhabitant of the wall said in a louder voice, "I'm sorry, Roger. You can come out from behind the cabinet. We are kind beings, but we know that when someone does something like that, and aggressively tries to break in for whatever reason, we must aggressively defend ourselves. We have no cops to call."

Grandpa regained his composure, ambled closer to the hole, and announced that he would fix it. He assured the being in the wall that he would speak to Jay about not revealing what had just transpired, but he also explained that he knew Jay well enough to know that he was a suspicious and fearful man, and that he would not discuss matters that bothered him for fear that those matters would come back to haunt him. He further explained that he was not like Jay—indicating that in many ways, he was the opposite. He explained that both he and

Grandma were curious types and loved to explore the unknown. Grandpa was trying to broach the inevitable: getting to understand the inhabitants of the walls.

"We know that," the voice said. "So are your granddaughters, Exi and Chel. Yes, we know all of you because we share our home with your shop. And Lyn and the girls are here often. But you don't know us. But I guess now you'll have to get to know us. We'll let you, Lyn, Exi, and Chel meet us. There are twenty-five of us here. But I want the four of you to meet only me at first."

"What are you? What do you look like?" Grandpa asked.

"All four of you will see me at the same time. I'll introduce myself and explain our overall appearance from within the wall—so you won't see me at first. This should hopefully soften the shock. Then I will step out to be seen, and we'll talk."

Grandpa had to ask, "Why are you living here in the walls?"

"Oh," the voice said. "Well, we were here long before you set up the magic shop. When those two weird anatomists were doing their experiments here, they created us. I mean, not like the miracle of human creation—these guys created us from human parts, genetic manipulation, and stuff. That was before they were arrested and sentenced to many years in prison for doing unethical and illegal experiments with human body parts.

"The crazy scientists built this building with extra wide walls and a wide ceiling, and they made several hidden doorways leading from inside the walls to the interior of the shop, and to the outside. They hid us in these walls, and specially engineered passageways and steps allow us to move around easily. The police cleared the place out, but they never thought to look inside the walls. Then you bought the place, so we just continued living here inside these walls and in the wide space between the first and second floor."

"Wow, this is hard to believe," Grandpa said. "But I have to believe it."

"By the way, my name is Dale and I'm president of our society: the Vs, like the letter *v*." A hand and arm reached out of the hole toward Grandpa; Grandpa took a step closer, and they shook hands. "I suppose it was just a matter of time before you discovered us. We tried to stay quiet when anyone was in the shop, but I guess we just got sloppy. We have become night 'people.' We hunt for bugs, worms, and certain plants; that's what we eat. Some seeds too, when we find them."

Dale interrupted himself. "Call your wife and grandchildren and see if they can meet here sometime today."

Since school was out for the summer, Exi, and Chel were free. All agreed to gather in the shop at noon for the mysterious meeting. Grandma explained to the girls' parents that they were going to view an interesting creature at the shop, but that they would be safe. Their parents agreed; Exi and Chel had participated in many unusual adventures with their grandparents, and all were safe and educational. On the way to the shop, Grandma told the girls what little she knew, but she successfully conveyed the message that they were going to experience something special.

◊

Grandpa welcomed Grandma and his granddaughters as they entered the front store area, and without hesitation, they all veered left for the door to the workshop. "Here's the hole that Jay made. In a few seconds, you will hear a voice from in there, and that voice will be from the president of a group of twenty-five beings who live inside the walls. There's nothing to be afraid of. He will tell us some things about themselves and then he'll come out to meet us. Okay?"

The three nodded while gazing at the hole.

Grandpa faced the hole. "Hi in there . . . Dale, you there?"

"Yes," Dale answered in his high-pitched voice.

"Oh my God! Wow!" Exi exclaimed.

Chel was expressing similar words of shock and backing away.

"Calm down," Dale said in a reassuring voice. "I don't bite. Come here, Lyn. I want to shake your hand."

As Grandma approached the hole, the girls covered their mouths with their hands.

A small arm and hand extended from the hole. "Hi, Lyn. It's nice to finally meet you," Dale said as they shook hands.

"Hi, Dale," Grandma said in return.

"Okay, girls." The hand beckoned Exi and Chel over.

After some eye and head contact that translated as "You go first," they sauntered over side by side and shook hands with Dale—the older, Exi, reaching out first.

"Okay, now that we've met . . . Well, you haven't met all of me yet. I have to explain my appearance before you see me. We Vs are mostly two arms. We stand and walk on our hands and arms, or we stand on one arm and do something else with the other. We have no legs or feet. When standing, we are shaped like the letter *v*—but upside down. The point where the two arms meet is up. We have small heads on top of the arms—about the size of a softball. But the lower part of our heads is actually a place where our other organs are located, a small stomach and so on. We are almost three feet tall and much more flexible than the usual type of human. Do you have an idea of what we look like now?"

Exi responded. "An upside-down *v* with a ball on top, right? I mean, the overall shape."

"Yes," Dale replied. "But we have cute round faces—no hair but lovely smiles and sparkling eyes. That's what you should look at first when I come out—my face—and then you won't be so frightened of our overall appearance."

Chel said, "Okay, I'm ready." The others agreed.

Dale said, "See the door that goes between the store and workshop? The part of the wall that meets the door when it's closed—the frame—well, the lower half of that is a door too. We can even open the regular door if we need to. There are seven doors that the mad scientists built in these walls, including doors to the outside. Oh, I'll explain the mad scientist stuff to Lyn and the girls later. Okay, I'll be coming out through the frame now."

Dale withdrew his arm from the room, and after a few seconds, the lower part of the frame opened, and Dale stepped out on his hands. All four did as he requested; they first looked at his smiling face. Then they gazed in amazement at his unusual form.

"Now watch me walk," Dale said, walking in a circle.

Grandma smiled and was the first to speak. "Dale, you are really kind of *cute.*"

All four were drawn to Dale. He was as charming as one could be.

This was the first of many meetings that were to transpire between four humans and the twenty-five Vs.

There was so much to talk about. The first discussion centered on ways to settle the living arrangements; it was agreed that the Vs would stay quiet during the day, and that they could stay in the attic apartment if they wanted, especially if it would be easier to remain silent. In fact, they made plans to insulate much of the attic floor over the store where customers would be; then they could move around and talk normally. The Vs loved the idea. Also, Exi and Chel agreed to bring them seeds occasionally to supplement their meals.

In return, the Vs promised to help Grandpa with his magic performances.

◊

"Ladies and gentlemen, introducing the greatest magician in the world, now in this wonderful Apollo Theater in New York City. Heeeere's . . . *Grandpa Magic!*"

Grandma, Exi, and Chel couldn't go to all his shows, and they were watching this one on TV at the grandparents' home.

The audience roared with delight and anticipation as Grandpa Magic came onstage walking on his hands, before propelling himself twenty feet in the air, rotating, landing on his feet, and announcing, "You ain't seen nothing yet. Watch this. You see that basketball hoop above me—higher than usual?" The audience looked up; it was thirty feet above the stage.

Grandpa Magic rotated 360 degrees, and when he again faced the audience, he held a basketball. He jumped off the stage and ran to the back of the theater, a distance far longer than a basketball court. He turned, faced the stage, and kicked the basketball far into the air. It sailed straight down through the hoop without even brushing the rim. Lo and behold, as it came through the hoop, basketball legend Michael Jordan was there to catch it, whereupon he announced, "Now *that's* the best shot I've ever seen." Again the crowd roared and loudly applauded. The show was off to a good start, and it maintained that momentum throughout.

Finally, the time came for the grand finale, and what many in the audience had heard about and come to see. Some well-known magicians were there to witness it and to try to figure out how it could be possible. The world of magic was befuddled by this magical performance. How in the world could Grandpa Magic make these props? He would never say. He had a good reputation for using only equipment that he made in his shop, a reputation he promoted, but the props he used in this last act were phenomenal.

Grandpa's assistant rolled a coffin to center stage. With the lid propped open, she and Grandpa tilted the coffin over so that the audience could view its interior as a beam of light revealed it. "Note that it's empty. And there is no room for a hidden compartment under its flooring," Grandpa announced as they closed the coffin and set it upright.

"Ladies and gentlemen, what am I removing from my right pocket? That's right, a *rattlesnake.* And what am I removing from my left pocket? You got it, another rattlesnake." Grandpa Magic's assistant opened the coffin. "I am going make these two snakes be nice." He tossed the twisting snakes into the coffin, and the assistant quickly closed it while scampering away. "Scaredy-cat, isn't she?" he announced. He waved his hands over the coffin and muttered some mysterious words. Then he turned to face the audience. "Now there are *no* snakes in there. They have joined together and have become an intelligent English-speaking being: a V." Grandpa Magic opened the coffin, and out popped the V, landing on the stage on his hands with his softball-sized head smiling at the audience. "Meet Dale," Grandpa Magic exclaimed. Dale stood on one hand and waved wildly to the audience with the other, yelling, "Hi, you all! Hi, you all!" The crowd roared.

The great Grandpa Magic tossed another pair of rattlesnakes into the coffin and out bounced another V; ultimately, a total of five Vs were dancing and laughing onstage. Near the end of the show, Grandpa Magic loudly asked, "Can a human create intelligent life? Oh, my precious little creations. Who wants to meet a V?" Hands flew up by the hundreds.

The five Vs jumped off the stage and skipped into the aisles, saying, "Hi, everyone, hi!" They each bounced on one hand to move around, shaking audience members' hands with the other. The most commonly heard words were some version of "They really seem alive!" Also, Grandpa Magic frequently heard words like "cute" and "sweet."

Finally, the Vs scrambled back onstage and the curtain closed, but the applause continued. The curtain opened again, revealing two Vs on each side of Grandpa Magic, now standing on their heads, and one V sitting on his head. All were flagrantly waving their hands, twisting from side to side, and laughing and yelling. Then the curtain closed; the great show was over.

◊

"That was *wonderful,* wasn't it?" Grandma exclaimed.

"Wow, it sure was," Exi said. "He's really made it big in the world of magic."

Grandma now raised a perplexing issue: "Do you two recall a moment when the camera focused on two men sitting together in the audience? They were preoccupied with something—not raving like the rest. Well, I recognized them. They're magicians. I think they were trying their best to figure out how Grandpa could create a V—to find out what a V really is. Magicians have even consulted with makers of puppets and makers of robots, but those people were just as perplexed."

"Yeah, I saw that," Chel said. "I was wondering why they weren't screaming like all the others."

Then all was quiet for a moment before Chel reflected once more on the show. "Grandpa . . . Grandpa Magic. He's such a great magician."

Exi softly said, "Yeah, because he's such a great pretender. There is a difference, you know."

Grandma agreed and solemnly said, "He *has* been a little brash lately, pretending he's on par with God. You could tell that by some of the remarks he made onstage. Did you hear him? 'Oh, my precious little creations' and such. And he's getting bolder. Sadly, I think he thinks he's foolproof; I'll be even sadder when his fellow magicians find him out."

◊

Grandpa was in a good mood as he opened the trunk of his car in front of the magic shop, singing his modified version of one of his favorite songs from his youth:

"Oh yes, I'm the great pretender / I seem to be what I'm not, you see / I pretend I'm a creator profound."

There was a three-week break before the next show; Grandpa could relax a bit. It was Sunday, so the magic shop was closed, and the family planned to have a picnic for the Vs at the shop—inside for privacy. Grandma and the girls scooted into the shop's store area to set up a card table for themselves and Grandpa, and to roll out some blankets on the floor for the Vs, while Grandpa was unloading sandwiches, salad, and sesame and sunflower seeds from the trunk. As Grandpa entered with the food, the twenty-five Vs filed in from various directions.

"Hi, you all," Grandpa said. "We're here to have fun and eat heartily. I was glad to learn that you Vs have discovered you can eat a variety of foods."

A loud *thud* came from the workshop. Mouths dropped; they all paused and turned to face the door leading there. Everyone quietly sauntered in that direction and cautiously entered.

They heard some noise from below the floor; it sounded like metal clanging, like clashing pots and pans.

Chel asked, "Grandpa, you don't have a basement here, do you?"

"No," Grandpa replied, now wearing a worried expression.

Grandpa turned to Dale. "Don't look at me," Dale said. "We've never heard a sound from under the shop. And we don't have access to whatever is below the floors."

"Wait, I smell . . . seems like . . . roast beef," Exi doubtfully announced.

Dale said, "Yeah, we smell that sometimes, rarely, when the shop is closed. Never knew what it was. Thought maybe it was some of Grandpa's chemicals. What's roast beef?"

Chel was now on her knees with her ears pressed to the floor. "Shh. I hear something. Something is setting a table with silverware down there. I can't *believe* this!"

As everyone became quiet, all could hear the sounds.

Grandpa looked upward and closed his eyes. *One of these miracles is perfect, but* please—*I can't handle another.*

Grandpa kept this poise for a few seconds, but he noticed that the silence persisted. He kept his eyes closed for a bit longer. He began to feel apprehensive about something. Then he opened his eyes and looked at Grandma. She was smiling at him. Everyone was motionless.

He looked at Exi and Chel. They were smiling at him too.

Everyone in the room was motionless and smiling at Grandpa. No one made a move or a sound; they were waiting for him to have the first word.

After a long hesitation, with the silent room full of smiles aimed at him, he realized there was nothing under the floor. The "perfect" magician being tricked triggered the self-realization that he was not magnificent. He sensed an unearthing on the part of the others that left him ashamed. It didn't take him long to realize that three of the people he loved the most, and his new buddies, the Vs, had to intervene on his false ways—on his airs of godliness—his presumed invincibility. "I . . . I *can* be tricked, fooled . . . I am a fool. I guess I *have* become a little . . . holier-than-thou." He looked sheepishly at Grandma and tried to force a smile, but his eyes swelled.

He knew why they all played a trick on him. A tear fell. He was glad he would no longer be the great pretender.

He knew this would have radical consequences. In his heart, he had known that eventually the jig would be up. Thank goodness it was due to his loved ones rather than the press or competing magicians.

In recent weeks, Grandpa began to realize that the Vs weren't some form of intelligent beings that simply lived in the walls. They *had* to live in the walls. He now recognized them as *human beings*. One thing he had felt good about was that now he was in a better position to help them as humans—innocent humans. They weren't clowns—not just props for magic shows so that Grandpa could be famous. They must decide their own destiny, and he could help them.

The thought struck Grandpa: *Is it possible to somehow delicately introduce them to society in a way in which they could be understood, so that they could live as other humans live? They are so different—but they are humans—very nice humans—just unusually shaped.* He impulsively proclaimed to the group, "Vs and everyone, do you know that you are *human beings?*"

As Exi and Chel were lifting a loose floorboard and removing the miniature recording device that Grandma had purchased at the spy shop, Grandma again faced Grandpa and made an announcement to the group: "Yes, we all know. Okay, now let's have some good ol' hot roast beef with gravy, and with carrots and potatoes! This food has passed the Dale taste test."

All the Vs jumped up and down, clapped, laughed, waved, turned cartwheels, and on and on—many jumping up and hugging Grandpa. What a show!

The End

ABOUT THE AUTHOR

Roger Grimson received a PhD in mathematics from Duke University and took an early retirement from the Department of Preventive Medicine and the Department of Applied Mathematics and Statistics at Stony Brook University, New York. He then started a statistical consulting business. He has published many professional papers in diverse areas: mathematical physics, biostatistics, epidemiology, and number theory, to list a few. But for many years, Roger wanted to be a fantasy fiction writer—so now he is.

Roger grew up in North Carolina and lived in New York for many years, but now he lives in Jupiter, Florida, with his wife, Linda, and their mysterious cat and three dogs. He has eight children and stepchildren—and many grandchildren.

Please address correspondence to:

Roger Grimson
4300 S U.S. Hwy #1 Ste 203-186,
Jupiter, Fl 33477